Crystal Gazing

Crystal Gazing

Jacqueline Wilson

An Armada Original

For Chris

Is There Anybody There? Crystal Gazing was first published in Armada
in 1990

Armada is an imprint of the Children's Division,
part of the Collins Publishing Group,
8 Grafton Street, London W1X 3LA

Copyright © 1990 Jacqueline Wilson

Printed and bound in Great Britain by
William Collins Sons & Co. Ltd, Glasgow

One

"Vicky! Wake up. Rachel, Tracy, come on, you sleepy lot. Time to get up," Mum calls, putting her head round our door.

I sit up in bed, yawning and stretching. My little sister Rachel is stirring, hardly able to move in her bed because she's got her old Cabbage Patch doll and her Care Bear and Her Little Pony and three tousled triplet Barbies all crammed under the covers with her. My big sister Tracy is still dead to the world, her magenta head half buried under her pillow. Yes, magenta. Tracy started work in a hairdressing salon last summer and she's still experimenting with all the hair dyes.

"I had such a weird dream last night," I mumble, swinging my legs out of bed. "I dreamt I thought all my skirts were much too short and so I let down all the hems."

"That wasn't a dream," says Rachel, sitting up too and starting the mammoth task of getting all her children dressed for the day.

"What?" I say – and then I grab my school skirt off the back of my chair and groan.

Rachel's right. It wasn't a dream. My school skirt had a huge hem too, so that now when I hold it up against me the skirt is practically flapping round my ankles.

"Oh no. What have I *done*?" I wail, and I rummage desperately in my part of the ward-robe. There's my good navy skirt – with its hem all unpicked and ragged. My red dress. My grey

5

skirt. Even my green and white check summer skirt. They've all grown an extra flappy bit at the bottom.

"It's going to take me hours and hours to sew them all up again – and I *hate* sewing. Rachel, why on earth did you let me?"

"I did try to stop you, honestly. But you said you knew best. You got quite stroppy about it. But then you played this lovely game with me and my dolls to make up for getting cross," says Rachel, lovingly clothing Cabbage Patch Clara in an old shrunken matinée jacket that used to belong to our little brother Craig.

"I played dolls with you," I say, sighing.

"And then you told me this wonderful fairy story," says Rachel happily, hugging Clara.

Tracy stirs, and makes pretend vomit noises.

"I always thought you were retarded, Rachel, still playing with your dollie-wollies now you're nine. But for you to be playing flipping fairies when you're thirteen, Vicky – that really takes some beating."

"You shut up, Tracy," I say, blushing furiously. "It wasn't my fault. I wasn't myself last night."

I mean that quite literally. I was obviously taken over by *her* again.

"Did I seem different last night? Talking in a funny way? Acting oddly?" I demand.

"Talking very funny. Acting extremely oddly. But then you always do," says Tracy. She suddenly shoots out of bed and makes for the bedroom door.

"Here! Don't you dare go in the bathroom. You always take such ages. You know I'm supposed to go first," I protest, dashing after her.

But Tracy is very fit from all the training for her women's football team. She streaks down the

6

hall and into the bathroom and I haven't got a hope of catching her.

"You should be a bit nippier," she says, slamming the bathroom door in my face.

I hammer and yell, but only half-heartedly. I'm getting really worried about this taking-over business. It's happening more and more. And it's so embarrassing. I start doing such crazy things. What am I going to do if Jen or Squirt come round after school and catch me playing dolls with Rachel like a little kid? They think I'm cracked as it is, because sometimes I get taken over at school and start spouting all sorts of stupid stuff that might impress the teachers, but makes all my form think me a right snivelling swot.

I don't know what I'm going to do. I can't go on like this. No one will believe me. They all think I'm acting a silly part. Or else they think I've gone really loopy. Mum got so worried she marched me off to the doctor's for a special consultation! Even Squirt, my sort-of boyfriend, said the other day that he doesn't know where he is with me at all. *I* don't know where I am. I don't even know *who* I am half the time. Most of the time I'm me, Vicky Smith. That's okay. I don't always think much of myself – I'm not especially clever or startlingly good looking or amazingly popular – but I've got used to myself, if you see what I mean. I can't get used to my *other* self.

I'll try to explain. Every so often I seem to get taken over by someone else entirely. It started when I held this joke seance in our loft with my best friends Jen and Karen and Alice. I was all set to play a few jokes on them and make them believe I was really in touch with the spirits of the past. But the joke

7

turned out to be on me. I really got taken over by this very pompous prim pain-in-the-neck Victorian girl. She calls herself Victoria Stathbridge and she insists she used to live in our road a hundred years ago. I somehow summoned her out of the past with my magical mystical powers.

It was Madame Rosalie who first drew attention to my special aura. She could tell right away that I'm a special psychic phenomenon. I have the second sight. I am a sensitive. Well, that's what she said, anyway.

I don't know what made me consult Madame Rosalie last summer holiday. I suppose I was feeling a bit fed up – the rest of the family were getting on my nerves at the time. So I took a stroll by myself along the pier and ended up inside her fortune-telling booth. She was so taken aback by my amazing aura that she offered me special psychic lessons, but I reluctantly refused due to lack of funds.

I wish Fairhaven wasn't so far away. If I could nip back and consult Madame Rosalie then maybe she'd be able to help me out of this ridiculous situation, find some way of making this irritating Victorian girl stay in her own times. I've got sick of her bobbing up in my body and taking me over. I think it's such a cheek. I'd never dream of flying back into the past and taking over *hers*.

I suppose we'll be going back to Fairhaven next summer but I'm not sure I can wait till then. Maybe I'd better try consulting a local fortune-teller. Only our grotty old town doesn't have a seaside with a pier, so I don't quite know where to find one.

When at long last Tracy deigns to come out of the bathroom I charge in and wash in a hurry, and then I shove on my school clothes, hastily pinning up my hem with safety pins. I run out of pins halfway round and have to make do with paper-clips. Luckily Craig is having a major tantrum because Dad needed a rag to wipe the cab window last night, and used the old flannel on the draining board that Craig had patiently planted with mustard and cress seeds that very day, and so Mum is far too preoccupied trying to calm them both down to notice my new steely skirt hem.

While I'm having my cornflakes I hunch up in a corner of the hall and try to look up fortune-tellers in our local telephone book. Would you believe it, not a single one! There's heaps of florists and foot clinics and funeral directors but no fortune-tellers at all. People are obviously desperate for carnations and corn plasters and coffins, but aren't a bit bothered about their future.

"Come on, Vicky, we'll be late."

It's my elder brother Robert chivying me. He's always desperate to get to school because he's so boringly brainy. He knows a million and one items of General Knowledge but he never knows anything *specifically* useful.

"Robert, do you know if there are any fortune-tellers living around here?" I ask, as we set off for the bus stop.

"Hurry up, Vicky. Fortune-tellers? Oh no, not *more* magic hanky-panky. You never know when to call it a day."

"I'm trying to make sure there's *less* magic hanky-panky," I say irritably. "Don't go so *fast*, Robert. The bus isn't even in sight yet."

But it's not the bus he's seen. He's spotted my completely barmy friend Alice, who has quite unaccountably got a crush on him.

"Quick!" Robert says desperately, breaking into

a run – but Alice catches us up at the bus stop.

"Hello, Vicky," she says, scarcely giving me a look. She turns her full attention to Robert. "Hello, Robert. I was so hoping I'd bump into you. I had such trouble with my maths homework last night. You're such a whizz at maths that I know if you'd just explain it to me I'd understand like a shot. Look, these are the questions." She waves the book under his nose, snuggling up as close as she dares.

Robert tries frantically to get away when the bus comes but Alice plonks herself down beside him, still gabbling away about maths, treating Robert like he's the wonderwhizz of all time. And it actually works a bit. Robert starts jotting down some of the answers for her, which is wickedly unfair, because he wouldn't help *me* one little bit when I asked him. I begged and pleaded but he was a right pig and just told me to push off because he had his own homework to do.

So I went off in a sulk and locked myself in the bathroom and eyed Robert's red toothbrush in the mug and wondered whether to wreak a terrible secret revenge by dunking it down the lavatory . . . and then Mum came up the stairs with Craig presumably tucked under her arm, howling his head off and obviously in some sort of mess . . . and Mum rattled the bathroom door and called, *"Is there anybody there?"* and then . . . then it started happening. And I spent the rest of the evening taken over by the Victorian girl.

I don't suppose she did anything useful – like my maths homework. I peer in my satchel and groan. I've just written down the questions. I haven't got a single answer. What am I going to do? We're supposed to hand in our homework first thing.

I crane round to see what Robert is writing out for Alice.

"Oh Robert, you're so clever," Alice gushes. "You make it all seem so easy. If only you were our maths teacher. You really have such a knack with figures."

Alice has quite a knack with her own figure too, wriggling around in the bus seat to show it off to the best advantage. Robert has gone bright red. He tries to calm himself by concentrating on the maths problem. He scribbles away, giving Alice more of the answers.

"Let's see," I say desperately, trying to lean across.

"Here! Do you mind? You're practically squashing me flat," says this large woman who's plonked herself down beside me.

"Well, could we possibly swop places? You see I need to see what my friend and my brother are doing and—"

"I'm not playing Musical Chairs just to keep you school kids happy," she says, and she simply won't budge.

By the time we get to school Robert's given Alice every single one of the answers.

"Tell *me*, Rob," I beg, as we pile off the bus. "It's not fair. I'm your flipping sister."

"Yes, it's a cross I have to bear," says Robert in a silly voice, and Alice giggles foolishly.

"Show me the answers, Alice, go on," I say, and I chase her up the school driveway, trying to catch hold of her book, which she keeps waving just out of my reach. She dodges in front of one of the teacher's cars. I dodge after her, making frantic grabs for the book. The car driver honks her horn indignantly.

"Vicky Smith! What are you up to?"

Oh no! It's Miss Raynor, our maths teacher! She's leaning out of her maroon Citroen and practically shaking her fist at me.

My brother Robert has completely disappeared. Never mind *me* being psychic. He can always sense when there's trouble brewing. Alice is doing her best to back away, but Miss Raynor comes bouncing out of her car and seizes hold of her too.

"Now, you girls. What's going on? You're too old for this silly sort of behaviour. It can be jolly dangerous barging in front of cars like that. Supposing my brakes were faulty? What were you doing?" She waits. We wait too.

"Vicky! Alice! What were you *doing*?" she repeats, working herself up into a right state.

"Nothing, Miss," says Alice.

"Don't be silly, Alice. You were both obviously engaged in *some* kind of activity," says Miss Raynor sharply.

"Yes," I say quickly. "We were . . . we were jogging, Miss Raynor. Getting a bit of exercise before school. Only we got a bit carried away."

"I think your imagination is getting a bit carried away now," says Miss Raynor, really getting into her stride.

There's a little audience gathering. We have become part of a public performance.

"Would you care to outline this jogging programme of yours, Vicky? And would you like to explain why every few seconds you ceased jogging and leapt up in the air, trying to grab hold of Alice's book?"

"Easy, Miss. I was getting in a bit of netball practice too."

My audience sniggers. I realize that humour was

12

an unwise tactic. Miss Raynor is getting very red in the face. Any minute now she'll be the same colour as her car.

"Could I see this token netball, please, Alice?" Miss Raynor demands.

"Oh. It's not a netball, Miss," says Alice, holding her book behind her back. "It's just a book, Miss."

"I know it's a book. An exercise book. And unless I'm very much mistaken I think it's a mathematics exercise book. Containing your last night's maths homework, is that right?"

"Yes, Miss," says Alice.

Miss Raynor finds the right page. She looks at all the questions. She sees all Robert's answers. He's used Alice's own smudgy biro, so that his usual neat figures are reasonably disguised. Miss Raynor nods, looking a little surprised.

"Well done, Alice. It looks as if you've come up with some very creditable answers. You were obviously listening in my class the other day." Her mood seems to have lightened and I relax a fraction.

This is a mistake.

"Vicky," says Miss Raynor, turning to me. "You seemed determined to seize hold of your friend's maths exercise book. Might I ask why? I wonder if you perhaps had difficulty with your maths homework, hmm? Maybe you haven't been able to come up with all the correct answers yourself?"

"Oh, I – I wouldn't exactly say that, Miss Raynor," I mumble, fidgeting.

The audience are grinning again. They can sense Miss Raynor is about to go for my jugular.

"Show me *your* maths exercise book, Vicky."

"My . . . ? Ah. Do you know, I'm not sure I've actually got it *on* me, Miss Raynor."

"Vicky Smith! Get your book out of your school-bag and hand it to me immediately."

I do so. Miss Raynor turns to the last page. She sees all the questions carefully copied out. She sees the huge gaps where the answers should be. She sighs and shakes her head.

"You didn't attempt to answer even one, Vicky!" she says.

"Oh, I did, Miss Raynor. I attempted them all. Sort of. But they – they momentarily defeated me. I wasn't going to hand my book in like that. I was going to try them all again before school."

"Vicky, I know exactly what you were going to do before school. You were going to grab Alice's work and copy down all her answers. Weren't you?"

"Oh Miss Raynor. Whatever gave you that idea?" I say, opening my eyes wide in assumed innocence.

It doesn't work. Miss Raynor takes my book and flaps it in my face.

"I can't stand cheats, Vicky. It's a stupid, pointless waste of your time and mine. Normally it would be an asinine act anyway, because Alice generally has about as much understanding of mathematics as you do. But for once Alice has bothered to listen and has tried to work things out for herself, with surprising success."

Alice gives a grin, though she looks a little shame-faced. As well she might.

"It's not your fault, Vicky, that you're so abysmally bad at maths – astonishing though this is, when I remember your brother Robert and his remarkable progress. If only you'd have come to me when I set this homework and explained that you felt it was beyond you, I would not have been at all cross." (I bet!) "I'd have gone through the questions with

14

you and tried to show you that they're really very simple indeed, if you'd only listen and pay attention. We had still better have this little consultation. Only now it can take place *after* school. You will stay behind and I will go through the questions with you, Vicky. You will answer them all. And then I will set you a further twelve questions to do at home tonight. Yourself. Unaided. Right?"

It is not at all right. It is all horribly wrong. I am absolutely furious with Alice, but she seems to think it's *funny*. And then to crown it all, the moment I set foot in the changing rooms for Games, Miss Harlston spots that there's something slightly odd about my school skirt.

"Vicky Smith! Come over here. What on earth have you done to your skirt?"

"Nothing, Miss Harlston," I say, trying out Alice's policy.

"Nothing! You're got practically an entire iron-monger's hanging from your hem. Half a dozen safety pins – and I don't believe it! Paper-clips!"

She picks up my skirt and waggles it about while all the others snigger. I'm getting sick of being the butt of all these teachers' jokes.

"You lazy girl! Why on earth didn't you sew it up properly?"

"I didn't have time. I only noticed it was like it this morning."

"Don't be silly. You must have noticed when you took your skirt off last night. You just couldn't be bothered. Why don't you try telling the *truth*, Vicky?"

There's no point trying to tell the truth. I can hardly say that most of yesterday evening I was taken over by a Victorian girl's ghost who's so stupidly prudish she tried to turn down all my hems, now, can I? So I let old Harlston nag on and on, still clutching hold of my skirt and exposing so much of my legs that if I were the Victorian girl I'd faint with embarrassment.

"I'm getting sick and tired of your attitude, Vicky. Look at the way you're standing there, not even bothering to reply. I can't stand dumb insolence."

It seems I just can't win!

"I'm sorry, Miss Harlston. I don't know what else to say. I'll get my skirt sewn up properly by next gym lesson."

"I think we'd better make sure it's decently sewn up sooner than that, Vicky. You can report to me after school. I'll provide you with a needle and thread and you can have your own private little sewing lesson."

"But Miss Harlston! I can't!"

"Oh yes you can."

"No, I mean . . . I've already got a detention for tonight."

"Good heavens! And this is just the first lesson! You're really excelling yourself today. What else have you got to do?"

"I've got to do some maths with Miss Raynor."

"I see. Well, I shall be here till five o'clock because we have a netball practice. So you can come along and find me after your little maths session and then get sewing. What a busy day it's going to be for you, Vicky."

This is getting ridiculous. I can't go on like this. I've *got* to get some advice from someone. I can't cope with this Victorian girl mucking up my life. It's all *her* fault about my skirt hem. If she hadn't pushed in where she wasn't wanted last night, then

16

maybe I'd have found some way of getting round Robert and getting him to help me out with my maths homework. I still can't credit it that he helped Alice like that. He always acts like he can't stand her. He runs in the opposite direction when he sees her coming. And yet when she's actually with him he goes all helpless, like a rabbit mesmerized by a stoat.

They even get together at lunchtime and wander round the playground together, Alice giggling and simpering and smiling up at my boring old brother. He doesn't seem to have much to say for himself. He busies himself taking off his glasses and giving them a good wipe.

"It must be love," my best friend Jen giggles. "He's getting all steamed up."

"I feel that way when I'm with Ian," says our other friend Karen. "I sometimes feel the atmosphere between us is positively electric."

"Yeah, I feel that way with Squirt – I keep getting nasty shocks," I say sharply.

"Yes, well, you and Squirt," says Karen disparagingly. "You're not exactly Romeo and Juliet, are you?"

"Imagine Squirt trying to climb up a balcony," Jen giggles. "He'd fall down before he was halfway up."

"Imagine Squirt spouting poetry," says Karen, spluttering.

"Imagine Squirt dressed like Romeo in those sort of romper things and *tights*," says Jen, and she and Karen double up with laughter.

"I'm getting a bit sick of your silly remarks," I say witheringly, and I wander off by myself.

I try to seek out Squirt, just for a bit of reassurance. It's not a good idea. I find him mucking around with a football with a whole load of his mates, and although he comes running over when I call him he doesn't look too pleased. All his mates jeer and scoff and whistle and make loud kissing noises.

"What is it, Vicky?" he says gruffly.

"I just wanted to tell you that I won't be able to walk home with you tonight. I've got a double detention. Maths and then I've got to do some stupid sewing. I'll be ages. It wouldn't be worth your waiting for me," I say – hinting, hoping that he'll do just that.

But Squirt takes me literally.

"Poor old you. Okay, I won't wait. We'll go somewhere tomorrow, eh?"

"I wouldn't necessarily count on it," I say huffily.

"Don't be like that, Vicky," says Squirt. "Come on, give us a smile." He starts tickling me.

"Stop it, Squirt!"

"Will you quit calling me *Squirt*? What's the matter with my proper name?"

"Okay – why don't you get lost, Jack Philip Andrew Norris? Go on, go back to your mates."

I have to face the lonely vigil of double detention unsupported. I spend a terribly gruelling half hour with Miss Raynor. She's trying to be ever so kind and patient at first, and tells me to speak up if there's anything I don't understand. So I speak up quite a lot and she stops being so kind and loses all her patience and I end up practically none the wiser. I'll have to go down on my knees to Robert tonight to help me out with all these extra sums she's given me.

Then I have to sit in my P.E. shorts, sewing up my stupid skirt hem. If *only* I could turn into the Victorian girl right now. She's probably a dab hand at sewing. I screw up my eyes and try like mad to will myself to be taken over, but nothing happens, and Miss Harlston comes bouncing over in her green flashes to ask me if I've got a pain.

I've got a real pain by the time I've finished my skirt. I've pricked my fingers so often they feel like pin cushions. It's getting very, very late too, and I get an uneasy feeling that Mum will be worried about me. Presumably Alice will have told Robert about my maths detention (and I hope he feels guilty about it too) but they won't know about the sewing session. I'd better give Mum a ring from the telephone box outside the school, just to let her know I'm safe and sound and on my way home.

Trouble is, this phone box keeps getting vandalized and I'm not sure if it's working properly or not. I put in my ten pence and dial, but first time round the phone just goes dead. I sigh and give it another go. Ah, it seems to be ringing now. I wait. Someone picks up the phone.

"Hello? Mum?" I say.

No one answers, though I'm sure there's someone on the other end listening.

"Is there anybody there?"

There's a sudden roaring noise, a rushing in my head. Oh no. It's happening again. I'm being taken over!

Two

Oh dear goodness! This is immensely irritating. I have been swept into the future yet once more, without so much as a by your leave. And at such an inopportune moment too! The kettle was just starting to bubble on the spirit stove and my mouth was watering at the thought of afternoon tea. An exceptionally good afternoon tea, because Great Aunt Louisa was paying a call. Mamma had therefore called for the bone china tea service, and asked for three kinds of preserve with the bread and butter, fruit bread and cherry loaf, and *five* different cakes, as Great Aunt Louisa has *such* a sweet tooth. I have a sweet tooth too, and I was happily contemplating trying a small slice of *each* cake – walnut and ginger, seed cake, plum cake, lemon madeira, and my special favourite and namesake Victoria Jam Sandwich.

But now I am hustled tea-less into the turbulent world of the future – and I do not even know where I am or what I am doing. I am in an unpleasantly small room with many glass windows. I am holding a strange gadget attached to a machine by a curious coil. For some reason I am pressing the gadget hard against my ear.

Oh my goodness! Manic laughter comes gushing out of the gadget, penetrating the very depths of my eardrum. I hold the gadget at arm's length, looking for its mouth. If it can laugh, perhaps it can also bite.

It has stopped laughing now. I can hear its voice. It's shouting and sqwarking in a very stupid fashion. It sounds very childish. I have heard little Peterkin burble many times in that irritating fashion. And the youngest Smith child – Craig – also specializes in idiotic loud noises.

"Craig!" it says suddenly.

I hold the gadget up in astonishment. Is it announcing that it too is called Craig? But its voice has changed. It is very little and tinny, and yet it is now unmistakably an adult voice. A voice that is cross and concerned. A mother's voice. A voice very similar to that of Vicky Smith's mamma.

"Mamma?" I say uncertainly, peering at the gadget.

It immediately bursts forth into a long speech, but most of it is such a tiny squeak I cannot comprehend it. Rather gingerly I bring the gadget nearer and then take courage and press it back against my ear.

"Oh Vicky, where have you been? I've been so worried, you naughty girl. Where are you now? Are you round at Jennifer's? Or is it that Squirt? Are you out with him?"

"Certainly not, Mamma," I say indignantly.

She seems to hear me perfectly. I cannot understand this at all. It seems unlikely that Vicky Smith's mamma *and* her obnoxious little brother have been transmogrified together into an ugly gadget in a glass-windowed box. It is equally unlikely that they are so reduced in size that they are hiding within the machine. My brother Leo is particularly gifted at ventriloquism, but he cannot throw his voice to this extent, nor give such an exact impersonation, albeit a much reduced and tinny version.

"You still haven't answered me, Vicky. Where *are* you?"

"I am not quite sure, Mamma," I say truthfully enough.

I peer out of the panes of glass. There is a very large and hideous building over the road which is grimly familiar to me. It is Vicky Smith's school. I have already paid one memorable visit there. It was worse than I feared. The children were very rough and uncouth and appallingly ignorant, and the teachers were little better, apart from a reasonably civilized gentleman teaching history. He specializes in the nineteenth century so we could have a very productive lesson. I like to think I have taught him quite a lot.

"*Vicky!* Stop messing me about. What do you mean, you're not sure where you are? Oh good lord, you haven't been abducted, have you?"

Yes, that is exactly what has happened to me. I have been wilfully abducted into the future – but I realize it is no use at all trying to explain this to Mamma. She is a kindly enough person, but none too bright.

"Calm yourself, Mamma," I say gently. "I think I have worked out where I am."

"Do stop calling me Mamma. It sounds so silly and affected. You know all that Victorian pretending gets right up my nose," says the Mamma.

I raise my eyebrows at the inelegance of her expression.

"Very well. I will not call you anything. I do not wish to offend you," I say obligingly. "I wish to put your mind at rest as to my whereabouts. I believe I am outside my school."

"Outside school! What are you doing there? Our Robert hinted you might have got a detention – but they'd never keep you this late. Oh Vicky, whatever have you been up to?"

"I'm sure I do not know. As far as *I* am concerned

my behaviour is nearly always exemplary," I say, irritated beyond measure that Vicky Smith has obviously been so wilfully naughty and stupid. If I am forced through circumstances to impersonate her from time to time then I do so wish she were a girl of a different calibre altogether, not this harum-scarum hoyden.

"Anyway, you'd better run for the bus now, and get yourself home as soon as possible," says the Mamma. "I don't know what your dad's going to say when he finds out. He thinks you need a good talking-to as it is."

"Indeed," I say haughtily. I do not care for Vicky Smith's papa at all. He is not a gentleman with a highly respected and profitable draper's establishment like my own dear papa. He is an uncouth man who drives a horseless vehicle of the future – and oh, how terrifyingly fast he drives it too! I fear he has a weakness for strong drink and even stronger language. My cheeks burn at the thought of this morally defective person giving *me* a scolding!

"I don't know *what* I'm going to do with you," the Mamma sighs. "You get yourself home."

"Mamma," I say. "Are *you* at home?"

"What? Well, of course I'm at home, you silly girl."

"Then pray tell me how I am talking to you with such ease. I cannot understand it. I gather Craig addressed me first in his own inimitable manner."

"Yes, well, you know what young Craigie's like. He *will* get to the phone first when it rings, and then he starts mucking about."

"The phone?"

"The telephone, you gormless girl!"

"Of course!" I am so slow-witted. I have heard all about this invention. It is Mamma and Papa's dearest

23

wish to become subscribers to a telephone exchange. Fancy! The humble Smith family have their own private instrument!

But just as I start a eulogy in praise of this now obviously commonplace invention it emits curious bleeping noises in my ear and then Mamma's voice is blotted out by a loud and unpleasant whine. I speak into the gadget but it refuses to reply. I therefore leave it dangling and attempt to extricate myself from the glass box.

"About time too," says an irate woman as I emerge. "And you haven't even put the phone back on the hook! You kids. Little vandals, all of you."

I stare at her, outraged.

"I am not a vandal, Ma'am," I say icily. "And I don't think it very civil of you to suggest such a thing. I will go straight home and tell my parents what you said. I am sure they will consider your assumption reprehensible."

"Miss Hoity-Toity," she says. "Have you swallowed the dictionary or something?"

"Just because I do not care to descend to the vernacular there is no need to mock," I say, and I sweep away, highly satisfied.

But I cannot help feeling a little lost and lonely nevertheless. I wish I could rush and tell my *own* parents about the rude woman. But Papa is now a hundred years in the past, supervising his staff at the clothing emporium, and dear Mamma is eating Victoria Jam Sandwich with Great Aunt Louisa, and I'm sure the boys will finish up all the cake and not leave a crumb for me. I will be suffering another of my recent "fainting fits" and will be lying unconscious in my darkened bedroom, and in the morning when I awake my "old" self, I shall have to face yet another visit from Dr Abbott and be dosed with his disgusting cleansing powders.

I sigh sorrowfully and then step out resolutely. I pass the post that I identify as a bus stop, but I am certainly not stopping for this bus. I have suffered a journey on a modern omnibus before and felt sure I was in mortal danger. I am certain the Good Lord did not intend us to hurtle hither and thither in such a manic manner. I will walk home to the humble Smith abode. The hideously ugly shoes that I am wearing seem stout enough and I can certainly stride out in this shameful skirt. I cannot understand it. I have a vivid recollection of adjusting the hem to render the garment a trifle more respectable. I shall adjust it once more the moment I am home.

The trouble is that I have not got a very clear idea which way home lies. All the buildings are so very different now. I cannot even work out which part of the town I am in. I see a church spire and make for it – but when I identify it I am more confused than ever. It is St Mary's – and we always call it St Mary's by the meadows. Many a time the boys and I have had merry picnics in the St Mary's meadows. I have waded in the brook and chased butterflies and picked cowslips to make into a fragrant ball. Now there is not even a blade of grass to be seen, and the very brook itself has bubbled its last. There are ugly slabs of buildings instead, many of which look like the clumsy constructions little Peterkin produces with his infant building blocks.

Constant traffic roars and rumbles past me and I flinch in fear, pressing myself against the walls, as far away from the kerb as I can manage. Once I hear a roar from above and I gaze upwards in astonishment to observe a machine flying right through the clouds, grazing Heaven itself. I point and gasp in wonder, and passers-by stare at me anxiously as if *I* am the marvel.

My footsteps get a little surer as I approach the town centre. I peer in the shop windows, though I wince at the inadequate displays. Sometimes there are scarcely nine or ten items within one window. Papa always prides himself on having at least a hundred artefacts on display at any one time, and the Stathbridge windows have become notorious. We often have quite a little crowd gathered outside at Christmas, when Papa decks the window with wreaths of holly and silver bells and glass baubles and little gilt angels, and every single item of stock on display is trimmed with scarlet ribbon.

I pause before another window, considerably shocked. It is some sort of ladies hairdressing establishment, but there are no curtains at all in the window to screen the communal abluting and arranging of the heads of hair. I see seemingly respectable women with wet hair dangling about their ears for all to see, women with curling devices hideously apparent, women with large bathing hats making a comical display of themselves. I tut in sorrow at such a scene – and then stare closely at a young girl with appalling purple-pink hair sticking up all over her head like garish feathers in a fan. How could these women let such a freak dress their hair? And then the apparition turns towards the window – and I realize who she is. She is Tracy, Vicky Smith's elder sister.

"Vicky!" she mouths, and then she comes to the glass door of the establishment. "What are you doing here?"

"I have been asking myself that precise question, Tracy," I say crisply.

"Does Mum know where you are? You know what an old worryguts she is."

"I have been communicating with her by using the telephone," I say proudly.

"Oh, you have, have you?" says Tracy, spluttering in a vulgar fashion.

"Tracy, dear. Don't forget your client," says a rather stout and formidable woman in a pearl grey costume. It is lamentably short, of course, but decently tailored, and I admire her lacy blouse with the large cameo at the neck. She is one of the few women of the future to appear adequately corseted too. She does not jiggle about in that lamentable manner when she walks.

Tracy pulls a silly face, but I feel her employer is correct to remind her of her duties. I give a little bob in apology, say farewell to Tracy and turn to continue on my journey.

"Wait a minute, dear." The lady in the grey costume is beaming at me. "You're Tracy's sister, aren't you? I'm Mrs Mortimer. I own the salon, dear."

I smile politely and hold out my hand. "How do you do, Mrs Mortimer."

She shakes my hand with a jingle of gold bracelets, looking surprised.

"What lovely manners, dear. Now. Tracy told me that you have quite a little talent for hairdressing yourself – when you're in the mood, she said." Mrs Mortimer glances at my hairstyle. Vicky Smith's hairstyle. "Only you don't seem to have been in the mood today, dear."

"Oh, she's in a funny mood all right," says Tracy.

"You go back to your client, Tracy poppet," says Mrs Mortimer, waving her hand at her. It sparkles with rings. Victorian rings. I stare at the garnets and turquoises on her fat white fingers, and give a wistful sigh when I spot the Regard ring on her wedding finger. "A Regard ring!" I say admiringly.

"That's right, dear. How do you know what it's called?"

"Oh, my Mamma has one very similar. Papa gave it to her on their first wedding anniversary," I say.

"What are you on about?" says Tracy. "Mum's never had a ring like that. Why is it called a Regard ring, anyway?"

"The initial letter of each stone spells the word Regard," I say. "Ruby, emerald, garnet, amethyst, ruby and diamond."

"That's right, dear. Tracy! Don't lean across your client like that. Now. What's your name? Vicky, is it?"

"I prefer Victoria, Mrs Mortimer. I do not really care for diminutive nicknames."

"Don't you, dear? I do so agree with you. My name's Nicolette, and yet I'm scarcely ever called it. And you can guess what they used to call me at school. Knickers!"

Tracy snorts with laughter and tries to disguise it.

"Tracy! Don't cough all over your client. She hasn't come here to breathe in your germs, dear," Mrs Mortimer sighs. "These girls! I try so hard to give them a proper training too, but sometimes I feel as if it's a losing battle. Now you, dear. Victoria. You seem to have an air about you. Natural lovely manners. You're just the sort of girl I could train up into a management position. Only of course you'd need a flair for hairdressing. And in spite of what your sister says you don't really seem to have that knack." She picks up a strand of Vicky Smith's limp hair and shakes her head.

I have no desire whatsoever to work in a hair-dressing establishment of the future, but I like Mrs Mortimer, and my pride is hurt.

"You must not judge me by the state of my hair at the moment, Mrs Mortimer. I have found that it is unpleasant to attend school with a carefully coiffed head of hair. It only encourages rude remarks from the vulgar element. But if I choose, I can dress it very differently indeed. Would you like me to show you?"

"Certainly. Oh, I do like the way you talk, dear. It's sweet music after the ugly slang one hears all the time from these modern girls. It's as if you've stepped straight out of the past."

"Thank you, Mrs Mortimer," I say, twinkling.

"That's what she's always making out – that she's some boring old Victorian girl," says Tracy. "She drives us all daft at home sometimes. Oh Vicky, what about Mum?"

"Oh dear, yes. I am afraid I should not stay after all, Mrs Mortimer. Mamma will be so anxious about me."

Mrs Mortimer raises her eyebrows and shakes her head.

"Such consideration! Why don't you telephone her, dear, and let her know where you are? I'm sure she won't mind. I know she was very thrilled when I offered Tracy here an apprenticeship. My salon has been in the town a long time, you know, and has an excellent reputation."

"Oh, I know how important it is to be attached

29

to a well-established firm with a good reputation. My papa has his own Fancy Drapers establishment, and he has worked so hard over the years to build up the firm's reputation."

"Really? I thought Tracy said your father was a taxi driver?" says Mrs Mortimer, looking puzzled.

"Oh! Yes, of course. I was talking about . . . the past," I say carefully.

"Oh, I see. Did he go out of business then?" says Mrs Mortimer, lowering her voice in sympathy. "Yes, these can be cruel times, Victoria. Anyway, dear, you ring your mother and tell her you're with me."

She gestures towards an object on her desk which is obviously her own personal telephone. I hesitate, not quite sure how to manage the connection.

"You haven't forgotten the number?" says Tracy, incredulously. "Honestly Vicky, you'll forget your own name next."

I will never forget my *own* name. I am Victoria Alice Mary Stathbridge, though of course no one here appreciates that fact. No one has any notion how intelligent and courageous and resourceful I am being, taking Vicky Smith's place in the future. I cannot even boast of my achievements and tell tales of the future when I am back in my own time. My experiences evaporate into hazy dreams, scarcely coherent, and the one time I tried to explain events to dear Mamma she became very anxious and I over-heard her discussing me with Papa, wondering if it might prove efficacious to send me to a Spa to take the water cure, as this has worked wonders for other young persons tormented by nervous delusions. I felt a little unnerved at this, and resolved to hold my tongue in future *about* the future. I do not care to spend my days in cold baths and hot mud, thank you very much.

Tracy recites the numbers and I click them out on the telephone.

"No, dear, take the receiver off first," says Mrs Mortimer. "I see you're not used to this sort of model. It's very simple really."

And so it proves. I am connected with the Smith establishment. The young child Craig gets to the telephone first and once more assaults my ear with manic screams, gurgles and cackles. That child could certainly do with a good whipping. Then at last the Mamma wrenches the receiver from his fist and we converse. She is perturbed at first that I am still absent from home – and astonished when I tell her that I am with Mrs Mortimer.

"But you've always said you can't stand it at Tracy's salon. You say the hairdressing smell makes your nose run and you can't stick Mrs Mortimer – is that her name? The bossy boots who owns the salon, her with all the jewellery."

I press the receiver tight against my ear to try to muffle Mamma's words. I smile brightly at Mrs Mortimer, who is standing by my side.

"I am going to demonstrate my hairdressing technique to Mrs Mortimer, Mamma," I inform her.

"You're *what?*"

I think the Mamma is laughing. There are certainly sounds of uncouth hilarity assaulting my eardrums.

"Goodbye, Mamma," I say, and put the phone down again, stroking the cream and gilt admiringly.

"You like my telephone, don't you?" says Mrs Mortimer. "We've only recently had this model installed. Your sister Tracy tried to talk me into having Micky Mouse phones – did you ever! I said, very novel for a toyshop, dear, but this happens to be a hairdressing salon. She's a very sweet girl, your sister, but she does have some silly ideas at times. Now! Are you going to do your hair for me, dear? You can wash it over at that basin. Use the lemon shampoo."

I blink at her, feeling rather insulted.

"I do not need to wash my hair, Mrs Mortimer. I do assure you, I keep it perfectly clean. I wash it every fortnight. And I do not use yellow soap nowadays. I find the yolks of two new-laid eggs more than adequate."

She looks amazed. I pat my locks to prove my point, but of course I do not possess my own long luxuriant curls. I am cursed with Vicky Smith's limp and lifeless tresses. Perhaps I had better try washing them with the lemon liquid soap after all. Mrs Mortimer assumes I was making some sort of feeble joke. She helps me with the rinsing and says I could do with a good conditioner.

"Alas, I am afraid I must agree with you," I say. "I do not generally care for pomades and oils, but certainly my scalp seems in need of stimulation. Mamma has her own recipe for such a lotion. She uses lime water and rose water, with a little eau de Cologne and glycerine."

"Really, dear? Yes, I've heard these old-fashioned remedies can come in very handy. Although I think I prefer something a little more up to date for my salon. Now! We'll towel you dry a little, and then you can show me your hairstyle."

"I really need some rag papers for the ringlets," I say.

"Won't curling tongs do, dear?"

The curling tongs do splendidly. I have no idea

how they work. They seem to heat up all by themselves – and very efficiently too. I am adept at using tongs, but I did once have a terrible experience with my fringe when I overheated my own implements.

For the ringlet style I dispense with a fringe altogether. I make a centre parting and comb Vicky Smith's hair vigorously to each side. I loop up the back into a satisfyingly round bun and secure it with pins that Mrs Mortimer provides. I am starting to attract a little audience. Tracy and some of the other hairdressing assistants are watching. I continue, attending to the ringlets now on each side of the ear. I make five fat ringlets on each side.

"Good heavens! How very distinctive," says Mrs Mortimer. "Whoever taught you to style in that fashion?"

"Oh, I just picked it up myself," I say demurely. Papa is a relatively wealthy man because his drapery is doing excellent business, but of course we cannot afford a proper personal lady's maid to attend to Mamma and myself. We have to acquire these little feminine arts ourselves.

"It's clever, yes – but what girl would ever want to go round looking like that?" says one of the hairdressers.

"I would," I say indignantly. "I think this is an exceptionally becoming style for a young girl just a little too young to put her hair up permanently."

"It would be lovely for a bridesmaid," says Mrs Mortimer. "Imagine Laura Ashley long frocks and this hairstyle. Oh, wouldn't it look a picture." She fiddles with my hair, working out exactly how to do it herself. "Ah yes, *I* see. Mmm. I think I shall have a go myself. Meanwhile, Victoria dear – how about you coming along to the salon on Saturdays, hmm?

I'm sure you'd be thrilled to have a little job and a chance to make quite a bit of money? I think we could manage – mm, five pounds?"

I reel backwards. Five whole sovereigns! I cannot believe it. Five pounds for a day's work – *every* Saturday! I would soon become richer than Papa! But common sense prevails. I seem to be able to hurtle backwards and forwards between centuries, but I do not see how I could take this money back with me. And it is no use Mrs Mortimer offering Vicky Smith this honoured position. Vicky Smith could not brush a hearthrug, let alone a head of hair.

"I am very flattered, Mrs Mortimer. But I'm afraid I'll have to think carefully about your offer – and discuss it with my parents."

"Very sensible, dear. I'm sure they'll encourage you to make the most of this opportunity." Mrs Mortimer stays excessively effusive, while Tracy finishes her client's hairstyle and goes to get her jacket. Mrs Mortimer waves her rings in the air and jingles her bracelets as she says goodbye.

"She's such a pleasant woman," I say, patting my impeccable hairstyle.

"Yuck!" says Tracy. "You don't know her like I do. And she's a crafty old boot. She's got no right to offer a kid your age a Saturday job – and for peanuts! Five pounds! She'd have you doing those ringlets all day long too, for brides and people going to posh parties and dances. You certainly impressed her though, Vicky. You are a weird kid. You've never shown the slightest interest in hairdressing and now all of a sudden you're doing all these fancy styles and setting yourself up as a proper stylist. If I didn't have my mind on higher things I'd feel a bit miffed." She hurries forward, starting to run.

I have to puff and pant to keep up with her.

"What are the higher things occupying your mind, Tracy?" I gasp.

"Football, of course," says Tracy, starting to run in earnest. "Come on, slowcoach. I've got to get in some serious training. We've got a big away-match on Sunday, our Ladies' Team."

"How . . . jolly!" I wheeze.

"Mm. We're going all the way to Fairhaven, to play some women's college there. There's some seats going spare on the coach. Want to come and cheer me on?"

"No . . . thank . . . you . . . Tracy. I . . . do . . . not . . . care . . . for . . . modern . . . coaches . . . or . . . cheering," I gasp, and then I have to stop, because my hairstyle and I are about to collapse.

Three

I mumble and sigh and groan in the sudden blinding glare.

"Bright light!" I mutter crossly.

"You sound like Gizmo," says Tracy, laughing. "Pity you don't look anywhere near as cute."

"Are you up already?" I say, screwing up my eyes.

"Oh boy, you're really bright as a button in the early morning," says Tracy, pulling on her tracksuit bottom. She hops nimbly on one leg, only stumbling when she lands on Rachel's Cabbage Patch Clara. Tracy lurches sideways, still only half in her trousers, and lands on top of me.

"Get off, you great lump!" I complain, swotting at her through the bedclothes. I catch sight of my alarm clock. "It's only half past seven – and it's *Sunday*. Are you mad, Tracy?"

"Not a bit mad. Fit, my girl. And raring to go." Tracy mock-jogs round the room, punching the air and kicking an imaginary football.

"Are you going training this early?"

"*No*. It's an away-match. A big day out. I *told* you. Oh, I do like to be beside the seaside," Tracy sings, flitting about the bedroom, gathering up her football gear.

"The seaside? You're going all the way to the seaside just to play football? And you won't even win, your team hardly ever do."

"They do so! Cheek!" says Tracy, practically garrotting me with her football scarf.

My screams wake Rachel. She doesn't come to

36

my aid. She gathers up her family instead, including poor trampled Clara, and tucks them safely out of harm's way into bed with her.

"We've had two away wins since I've been put in the team," says Tracy indignantly. "And today's going to be the third, just you wait and see, Vicky. That Fairhaven Women's College sound a right weedy lot, a load of brainy bookworms who can't kick a ball for toffee—"

"Fairhaven!" I say, and I sit bolt upright.

"Mmm. Well, wish me luck, you two."

"Good luck, Tracy," says Rachel. She makes Clara nod her head and wave her arms. "Good luck, Tracy," says Clara, in a squeaky version of Rachel's voice. Then she picks up the number one Barbie. They all start chattering "good luck" in dollygirl voices.

"Shut up, Rachel," I say, leaping out of bed. "Oh Tracy, you pig. Why didn't you tell me you were going to Fairhaven?"

"I'm not talking, Vicky, it's Barbie-two. And now Barbie-three will have to say it too, or else she'll sulk all day," says Rachel in aggrieved tones.

"I told you I was going to Fairhaven. I even offered you a seat on the coach," says Tracy huffily.

"You didn't! And I've been dying to go to Fairhaven. I urgently need to consult Madame Rosalie."

"What, that fortune-telling lady? Don't be daft, Vicky, she's the one who made you go completely bonkers. You've been edging towards lunacy ever since you were a little kid, but that Madame Rosalie tipped you right over the edge if you ask me."

"Tracy, did you *really* ask me about going to Fairhaven? *When?*"

"I don't know. Yes, I do. It was the day you

37

came round to the salon and showed off doing all the ringlets. Mrs Mortimer was dead disappointed you didn't turn up yesterday. She had a client going to a posh party on Saturday night and she wanted a new hairstyle that would really make her stand out. Mrs Mortimer thought your ringlet job would be just the ticket."

"If I'd done her hair yesterday her client would have an incredible bird's-nest hairstyle that would *really* make her stand out," I say. "I tell you, I wasn't myself that day. Don't you remember, I let down all my skirt hems *again*. Please, don't ever let me get near a pair of scissors in future, no matter what," I gabble, tearing around the room, flinging on the first clothes I can find.

"That's *my* sweater. Get it off!" Tracy commands. "Why are you getting dressed?"

"I'm coming too! To Fairhaven."

"Oh no you're not."

"But you said I could. You said I could have a seat on the coach."

"I said that *originally*. It's too late now. All the seats have been taken. Friends, brothers, boyfriends, one or two of the mums. There isn't a seat left, Vicky. You're too late."

"No, I'm not. I don't need a seat. I'll sit on the floor. Sit on your lap. I'll even squash into the boot with all the football kit. Just let me go to Fairhaven with you. Please. I'll cheer and cheer and cheer, I swear I will."

Tracy sighs. "Oh, I don't know. Maybe we can all squash up together on the back seat. Yes, all right. If Mum doesn't mind."

"Can I come to the seaside too? And Clara? And Carebear and My Little Pony and Barbie-one

38

and Barbie-two and Barbie-three?" says Rachel. "I can get us all dressed in a tick, you'll see. We want a day at the seaside too."

"Rachel, I'd take you ordinarily, but I can't lump you along to Madame Rosalie too. I need a private consultation. Sorry. It's vital, you see. I've got to get myself sorted out one way or another."

"Well, I can see you certainly need to do that," says Tracy. "Come on then. A bit of breakfast, and then we'd better get cracking."

I charge along to the bathroom and then rush downstairs to stuff myself with cornflakes. Mum appears in her dressing gown with Craig clinging to her hip like a very large limpet.

"What are you doing up, Vicky?"

"I'm going to Fairhaven with Tracy."

"I don't know about that," says Mum doubtfully. "What are you up to, eh? I never know where I am with you nowadays, Vicky. You're not the slightest bit bothered about this ladies' football so why do you want to drag off to the seaside with them?"

Luckily Craig hears the word "seaside" and starts clamouring that he wants to go too. He's nowhere near as easily put off as Rachel. He begs, he whines, he starts howling – and he's still at it when Tracy and I leave the house.

"Thanks a lot," says Mum grimly. "He'll be in a right mood all day long. Oh well. You two enjoy yourselves. I hope you play well, Tracy. And keep an eye on our Vicky for me. Don't let her wander off by herself, eh?" Mum suddenly thinks. "Here, you're not going near that Madame Rosalie, are you, Vicky?"

"Sorry, Mum?" I say, belting down the garden path, making out I can't hear her.

"Vicky! Come back here. You're *not* to start up any more of this occult hankie-pankie, do you hear me?"

I waggle my ear in a hopeless way to indicate that I'm not hearing her at all, and then I smile and wave and run for it. Tracy runs with me, her kit bag in one hand. She soon outruns me in spite of the bag.

"Wait for me, Tracy. Oh no. I've suddenly thought. I've come out without any money."

"You don't need any. We get free nosh. You can share mine if there's not enough to go round, but there's usually heaps. They know we've got big appetites."

"No, it's for Madame Rosalie. I'll need something for my consultation."

"I thought you just this minute promised Mum you wouldn't go near her?"

"I didn't say a word. I've *got* to see her. Oh Trace, lend us five quid, eh?"

"You're joking! I haven't got it, anyway." Tracy slows down and puts her hands in her jacket pocket, bringing out a few coins. "Here. About a couple of pounds, that's all. In case we stop for a drink on the way back."

"Oh well, it's better than nothing. Maybe she'll do a reduced rate again," I say, holding out my hand for the coins.

"Get away. I *said*. This is my drinking money."

"Oh come on. Footballers can't drink. You've got to keep fit. You don't want a beer belly."

"I don't think a lemonade shandy is going to do me any lasting harm," says Tracy, but she tosses me a pound coin. "Here. You can cross old Madame Whatsit's palm with this if you like.

It's out of season so she'll be glad of any offering."

"I hope so. She did give me a consultation before at a cheap rate. Because I'm a sensitive, you see. She could tell at once there was something very strange about me."

"Yeah, that's most people's reaction when they meet you, Vicky," says Tracy, pulling my hair. "Look at the state of this!"

I've scragged it back into a lop-sided pony tail without even brushing it properly.

"Well, I was in a hurry, wasn't I?"

"And you're Mrs Mortimer's blue-eyed girl of the moment. She'd change her tune fast enough if she could see you now."

"I don't ever seem to stay anyone's blue-eyed girl for long," I say, sighing.

"Because you keep messing people about. Chopping and changing. Acting brilliant at a thing one moment and hopeless the next."

"Exactly. That's why I need to see Madame Rosalie. So she can stop all this messing about, as you put it. So I get stuck as one person. Me."

"And which one's that?" says Tracy, laughing at me. "Is the real Vicky Smith brilliant or hopeless?"

"Hopeless, I suppose," I say. "Still, I think it's better to be consistently hopeless, don't you, Tracy?"

"I don't really know what you're on about. I never do nowadays. But I can't see why you can't ask this Madame Rosalie to make you consistently brilliant. That would be a better bet altogether."

"You don't understand," I say. The only way I could do that would be for me to swop places altogether with this girl from the past and of course I'd never ever do that!

There's a whole crowd of beefy athletic girls bouncing around waiting for the coach. Some of them look so powerfully built I bet they could jog all the way to Fairhaven and still manage a full game of football. One great golden girl positively towers above her boyfriend. He's small and short with fair spiky hair – and when he turns round I give a little gasp. It's Squirt! I can't believe it. I know we had a bit of a tiff the other day but that's no reason to start two-timing me. And what's he doing with an Amazon like that anyway? She looks like she could pick him up and juggle with him one-handed.

"Hey, Vicky!" Squirt calls.

What a cheek he's got! He doesn't even look bashful.

"Isn't that Squirt?" says Tracy. "What's he doing here, Vicky? Is he with Ann? She's our new substitute."

"I don't know and I don't care," I say savagely, and I clamber up into the coach.

There's a great crush and I have to squash up with Tracy and Tracy's friend Sue. Sue is a nice enough girl, I suppose, but she's thirteen stone of solid muscle. Squash is the operative word. Every time the coach turns a corner I go flying into the aisle. I'm in mortal fear of Sue tumbling after me and landing on top of me. I don't want to be steam-rollered.

I'm feeling pretty flattened as it is, seeing as Squirt is here with this other girl. She's quite good looking – if you care for that over-blown, obvious type of curvy blonde. Goodness knows what she sees in Squirt. Well, she's welcome to him. They're sitting right up at the front but he keeps turning round in his seat and yelling things at me. I can't hear what he's saying. And as if I care anyway. I yawn ostentatiously.

"Did you get up too early, Vicky?" says Sue, turning to me.

"Mm? Oh no," I say, clinging to my square inch of coach seat.

"I didn't know you were a football fan. Are you hoping to join the team eventually?" she asks earnestly.

Tracy snorts with laughter.

"Our Vicky has trouble running for the bus. No, she's just here because she wants to go to Fairhaven."

"Oh yes," says Sue politely. "Like the seaside, do you? Pity the sun's not out. In fact it looks horribly grey and foggy. I think we're going to need miners' lamps strapped to our foreheads to get a proper look at the ball. How do you reckon we're going to do, Tracy? Do you think we've got a chance of beating them?"

"Of course we have. But don't ask me. Our Vicky's the psychic one of the family. Are you any good at clairvoyance, Vicky? Whip out your crystal ball and tell us what's going to happen."

"I predict you're about to experience a sharp pain in the region of your waist," I say, and I give her a dig in the ribs with my elbow.

"Ow! Cheek! Right, Sue. Let's lean on her."

"No! Okay, okay, I'm sorry. I'm grovelling. And gosh, I'm getting a clear picture in my head of this afternoon's football match. Yes! You've scored a goal, Tracy. And you too, Sue."

"I hope it's not an own goal. I'm the flipping goalkeeper," says Sue. "Are you really clairvoyant, Vicky?"

"That's why she's coming to Fairhaven. To have a special consultation with Madame Rosalie, this fortune-teller on the end of the pier," says Tracy. "Only as it's my money paying for this famous consultation, I want any predictions about tall dark handsome strangers to be reserved specially for me, okay?"

"Do not mock the occult arts, Tracy," I say haughtily. "I have serious matters to discuss with Madame Rosalie. I'm not going to waste the consultation asking if my sister is going to meet a tall dark handsome stranger."

I am so eager to see Madame Rosalie that I don't even hang around for the free grub when we get to Fairhaven at last. I decide to go and consult with her without delay.

"Okay, I'll save you a sandwich or something," says Tracy. "Come back in time for the match, eh? We need all the support we can get."

"You bet," I say, and I march off purposefully.

"Hey, Vicky! *Vicky!*" It's Squirt again. He comes running after me. "What's up with you? Why are you acting so funny? You're practically ignoring me."

"Go away, Squirt," I say, swotting at him.

"Where are you going?"

"Mind your own business."

"Don't be like that, Vicky. I don't know what I've done to annoy you. I was dead chuffed when I saw you were coming today. Come on, come and meet Ann. She's just getting her gear out of the coach."

"I don't want to meet her, thanks very much," I say, outraged. "If that's the sort of girl you want then good luck to you. Now leave go of me. I've got things to do – very important things. So you push off

44

back to this Ann girl. Look, she's waving to you to come and help her."

Squirt is staring at me. And then a little smirk creases the corners of his mouth.

"You're jealous!" he says.

"Of course I'm not jealous! I don't care if you go out with the entire football team, my sister Tracy included. They're welcome to you, you silly little Squirt," I say, and I start running.

He runs after me for a bit but he soon gives up and goes off to join Amazon Ann. I run on, not stopping until I get right to the seafront. It's much cooler and foggier nearer the sea. That's probably why my eyes are watering. The pier looms out of the mist like the skeleton of a vast sea monster. Perhaps Madame Rosalie might help me sort out my love life as well as my psychic possession problems.

I step out on to the creaking wooden planks of the pier. I pass the ice cream booth, the doughnut stand, the fresh shrimps and winkles stall. And then I stop dead. Because I can't go any further. There's a barrier right across the main part of the pier. I blink through the mist. I read the sign. CLOSED FOR THE WINTER.

I feel like screaming. I stand and rattle the barrier in frustration.

"Now then, Missie," says the winkle man, shaking his head at me.

"But I want to go on the pier! I didn't realize it shut for the winter."

"We're open, Missie. Treat yourself to a nice plate of winkles."

"I don't want any winkles, thanks. I want Madame Rosalie," I say miserably.

"Oh. You want your fortune told, do you?" says the winkle man.

"I came all this way to Fairhaven – and now she's not there. It's all shut up. And I don't know what to do," I wail, nearly in tears.

"You want your fortune told, so why not have a go on that machine over there?" says the winkle man helpfully.

He indicates a silly slot machine with a puppet dressed up in a scarf and shawl, hunched over a goldfish bowl. I don't think it's going to be the slightest help, but I get him to change Tracy's pound for me and then I shove ten pence in the slot. The puppet shakes, the goldfish bowl glows, and then a pink card comes out of the slot at the bottom.

It says two words. HARD LUCK. I give a hollow laugh.

"That's it. You cheer up, Missie. Here, have a winkle. On the house."

I'm starving hungry by this time so I give a winkle a go, although I've always thought they look very dubious indeed. They taste dubious too. Yuck! I'd give anything to spit it straight out, but I don't want to hurt his feelings, especially as it was a gift.

"I wonder what Madame Rosalie does all winter," I say, sighing.

"Old Rosie? Her old man has a fruit and veg stall at the corner of market street. I think she helps him out while he has a bit of a warm down the *Dog and Fox*."

"Really! Oh goodness. I could go and look for her there then," I say excitedly.

"Well, you could do. Of course, you won't find her, or her old man. Not today. It's Sunday, isn't it.

Only us seafront stalls are ever open on a Sunday. Another winkle?"

"No, thank you very much."

"Of course, if you're really wanting to see her, like, you could go round to her home."

"You know where Madame Rosalie lives?" I say breathlessly.

"Mmm, think so. Victoria Terrace, isn't it? Number 6, number 8, somewhere round there. It's up on the hill, overlooking the sea. Very nice views, only Rosie and Stan have got a basement flat so I don't think they'll see much."

Victoria Terrace! The very name seems a good omen. I thank the winkle man enormously and make for the hill. The fog is getting thicker and there's a horribly depressing drizzle but I'm not going to let myself get down-hearted. I don't see how Tracy and Sue and all the others are ever going to play their game of football if the weather stays like this. Still, that's their problem. *My* problem is getting Madame Rosalie to sort out my psychic powers and get some sort of order into my occult adventures.

It doesn't take too long to find Victoria Terrace, although the fog is so thick now that I can only see a few feet in front of me, and the famous sea view is just a blank white wall of mist. I don't even have any difficulty finding the right number. There's a special little placard on the basement door of number 8.

Madame Rosalie. Fortune-teller to the famous. Of genuine gypsy origin. Private consultations. Hand-readings, tea leaves, tarot, crystal ball.

I can feel myself tingling with excitement. It must be evidence of my psychic powers revving up for Madame Rosalie's inspection. I hurry down the basement steps and ring the doorbell. There's a wonderful smell of roast Sunday dinner that momentarily distracts me.

She's a long time answering her doorbell. And yet I can smell her cooking so she must be in. I ring again, loudly and determinedly. At last I hear footsteps in the hall. The door opens and a fresh waft of wonderful roast beef and Yorkshire pudding makes me faint with longing.

"Yes?"

I stare at the old lady in her pink knitted jumper and baggy trousers and smile in intense relief. It's my Madame Rosalie at last, even though she's not wearing her gypsy scarf. She looks as if she's been wearing it recently, however, because her little grey curls are squashed flat against her head, like pressed flowers.

"Oh Madame Rosalie, I've found you!"

"What do you mean, you've found me? I haven't been in hiding," she says, chewing.

"No, I mean, I went to look for you on the pier and it was all shut up and I got so upset but then this winkle man – well, anyway. I've come for a special consultation."

"Oh no you haven't. It's Sunday. I never give special consultations on a Sunday. And I'm in the middle of my dinner too. So you run along, dear, and we'll fix something up another time."

"Oh please! It's desperately urgent. I *can't* come another time. I live miles and miles away. I could only come today because I got a free seat on my sister's football coach – well, I didn't get a seat at all actually, I had to squash up with her and her friend . . . Anyway, I *must* see you. I have

48

this terribly urgent psychic problem, you see, and you're the only one who can help me."

"Well, I told you. I don't give special consultations on a Sunday. Especially when my lovely Yorkshire pudding's going cold on my plate. However . . . I can see you're desperate. So if you pop back in an hour or so I *might* just be able to accommodate you as a very special favour. But it will be double rates, of course, seeing as it's a Sunday. Twenty pounds."

"What!"

"Twenty pounds, dear – and there's many a fool pays far more than that just to be told a lot of rubbish. I'm the best, dear. Very famous people consult me. Including a very highborn famous person indeed. Need I say more."

"But your special rate was five pounds in the summer, and if you double that it's ten pounds. Not twenty," I say wretchedly.

"Well, I've got to put my rates up occasionally, dear. You don't want me to starve, do you? Which I am, right this minute. Make up your mind. Are you coming back or not?"

"Not," I say. "I haven't even got five pounds, let alone twenty. I've got about a pound's worth of change here, that's all. No, I spent ten pence of that on a slot machine."

"Well, we're wasting each other's time then, aren't we?" says Madame Rosalie, and she goes to close the door.

"Don't you remember me?" I say frantically. "You said I had fantastic occult powers, that I was a true sensitive. You said my aura was so strong it almost blinded your psychic eye."

"I said that, did I?" says Madame Rosalie, pausing.

"And you're absolutely right. I didn't know it up till then. But you set me thinking. And messing about with the psychic world."

"You should never mess about with psychic powers, dear," says Madame Rosalie, drawing in her breath with a disapproving hiss.

"Yes, I know that now. Because it's all gone horribly wrong. I'm possessed, Madame Rosalie."

"Are you?" she says warily.

"Not right this minute. But often. And I can't control it. It all started when I did this seance thing with some friends from school and I tried to summon up a spirit."

"Amateurs never come to any good," says Madame Rosalie. "You can't go holding seances just like that. You need years of training. You should have come to me for instruction."

"Yes, but I couldn't afford to. And anyway, this girl from the past, she took me over. It was so strong I couldn't stop it happening. She just sort of overwhelmed me and I started speaking like her and acting like her. Everyone thought I was messing about but I swear I wasn't. I wasn't me any more. I was her."

"Remarkable," says Madame Rosalie, sounding reluctantly impressed. "Perhaps if you care to pop back you might give me a demonstration? We'll negotiate a special rate just for you. I'd never like it said that Madame Rosalie haggled over money matters."

"Yes, but I don't think I can do it to order. That's the trouble. I can't start it – and I can't stop it either. I can't stop her. She keeps taking me over and stirring things up and making a fool of me – and I just can't stand it any more. I want you to help me get rid of her once and for all. Because it's driving me crazy."

I'm feeling crazy too, desperately pleading on these foggy basement steps. The smell of food is so strong that I can barely concentrate any more. The fog seems to be thicker than ever. Madame Rosalie's pink jumper has gone fuzzy, her flattened curls have started stirring. The steps underneath me start to shake.

"Oh no, what's happening now?" I wail – and then the fog envelops me totally.

Four

The fog slowly clears. I blink my eyes, shake my head, try to sit up.

"You'd better stay where you are for the moment, dear."

"But where am I?" I swallow. '*Who* am I?"

"Well, I don't know your name, dear. You've yet to introduce yourself." A face looms in front of me.

I recognize those flattened curls. I lie back limply in her pink woolly arms, weak with relief.

"Oh thank goodness. I'm still me, Vicky. Still here. So what happened?"

"I think you fainted, dear. Perhaps because you were getting so agitated. And when did you last eat, hmm?"

"Breakfast," I say sadly. "I could have had a sandwich with my sister, but I didn't bother because I was so eager to see you."

"Really, dear?" says Madame Rosalie, sounding pleased. "And you've eaten nothing since breakfast, eh?"

"Well, I had a winkle."

"I don't think one winkle's going to fill you up. Right. When you've come to yourself a bit, we'll take you indoors and see if we might rustle up a spot of lunch."

"Oh please!" I say, too desperate to toy with polite refusals.

Madame Rosalie helps me into her kitchen. There's a man eating his Sunday lunch in an alcove by the window. He nods at me calmly and carries on chewing, as if he's used to frantic females fainting on his doorstep every day of the week. Madame Rosalie whips out a fresh plate and scrapes round the vegetable tureen while her husband – Monsieur Rosalie? – cuts me several slices of roast beef from the joint.

"There. You tuck in to that. And have a piece of my Yorkshire too – that'll perk you up if nothing else will."

I eat with enormous enjoyment. I feel so much better that I manage to stop concentrating so completely on my plate of food and start peering round the room. I hope to find painted stars on the ceiling, astrological signs on the wallpaper, weird velvet hangings, crystal balls on the kitchen dresser, but it all looks very ordinary, just like our own kitchen at home.

When I've finished every scrap of my meat and veg Madame Rosalie insists that I share a huge bowl of fruit salad too.

"It's all fresh fruit from my Stan's stall. The very best quality. You look as if you could do with some vitamins. Still, if you've been meddling unduly with the spirit world, that can weaken your constitution something dreadful. Even seasoned specialists like myself have to learn to ration their sessions. Fortune-telling and palm readings, they're not too draining, but if I'm actively attempting communication with a departed spirit, well, dear, I'm completely shattered afterwards. I'll only do one of those specialist jobs once a week, and even then I have to make sure I have a good lie down afterwards."

"I don't *want* to meddle unduly, Madame Rosalie. Not now. But I can't seem to help it. Sometimes it

53

happens three or four times a week, there's just no stopping it."

Madame Rosalie sucks in her breath.

"Oh goodness! No wonder you're looking drained. I can see why you felt compelled to track me down. Did you know, Stan, this kiddie's travelled a long way to see me, and then traced me from the pier, acting like a little detective. See. She could have consulted many other spirit mediums, but she knew she had to opt for the best."

"That's right, girl," he says, stretching and sighing. "Well, I don't know much about the fortune-telling lark, but you don't need to be clairvoyant to know you're a smashing cook, Rosie. Your Yorkshire's positive food for the gods. I think I'll go and digest it with the care it deserves."

He gets up and goes into the living room. After a minute or two we hear the deep rhythmic snores that are an obvious by-product of his "digestion".

"We'll just clear the dishes, dear, and then we'll have a proper consultation," says Madame Rosalie.

"But I still haven't got anywhere near enough money. I get £1.50 a week pocket money – I could write you out an I.O.U. and then send you your fee in installments," I say.

"I daresay we'll sort something out. Now. Let me get things clear. This girl from the past who keeps materializing. Is she within you or is she a separate psycho-plastic full-form materialization?" Madame Rosalie sees my blank look. "Do you notice a strange vapoury substance, dear? A bit like the fog out there. And does it collect and become an actual psycho-plastic mould, and you step into it and direct it, communing with the soul from the past?"

"Oh no, it's not like that at all."

"Pity. I've read about these cases and I've always fancied seeing one. There was this charlatan lady of my acquaintance, she kept insisting she had all these psycho-plastic transfiguration experiences, even got her hubby to photograph her looking all white and misty, but when she gave an actual demonstration we soon found her out. Do you know what her psycho-plastic spiritual essence was? Shaving foam." Madame Rosalie tuts disgustedly as she does the washing-up. "It's women like that who make life so difficult for the rest of us. We true psychics." She smiles at me. I smile back, feeling flattered.

"So, dear. You go into a trance, is that it?"

"I . . . I think so. But I can't work out why. Something obviously triggers it off. The first time it happened there was a big thunderstorm, but there's been another storm since and it didn't happen then."

"Still, the weather is often very influential. I always listen carefully to what Michael Fish has to tell me. Sun or storm, it can make all the difference to a psychic experiment." Madame Rosalie peers out of the kitchen window. "Of course, I'm not sure about fog, as such. Still, I suppose you could say it's a symbolic manifestation of the mists of time. Use the white tea towel for the glasses, that's a good girl."

We deal with the washing-up speedily and then Madame Rosalie prepares for our consultation. She puts her head round her living room door.

"Normally I hold my little sessions in here, dear," she says. "But I don't think the ambience would be right just now, not with my Stan having his forty winks. So you'd better come in the bedroom."

Madame Rosalie is obviously very fond of pink. The wallpaper's pink roses, the carpet is deep pink swirls, the wardrobe and dressing table are pink gloss paint, and the old-fashioned, silky eiderdown on the bed is quilted in three shades of pink, with a pink poodle nightdress case curled up on her pillow. The ambience doesn't seem quite right in here either, but Madame Rosalie draws the curtains so we're in a dark pink gloom, and spreads a crimson velvet cloth over a little bedside table, first removing a packet of dental fixative, an alarm clock, a bag of humbugs, and several Catherine Cookson paperbacks. She carries the cloth-covered table into the middle of the room, and then goes to a chest of drawers and brings out another velvet cloth. She unwraps it very carefully and produces a crystal ball. Aha! She places it reverently on the table, and then holds her hands to it, as if it might give off warmth. It glows in the darkened room like a pale moon.

Madame Rosalie then beckons to me. I shuffle forward across the carpet, my heart beating faster.

"Kneel down, dear, and put your hands on the table," she commands.

I do as I'm told. Madame Rosalie does likewise, though her kneejoints crack loudly and she gives several groans before she gets comfortable. She puts her hands on the table too, her fingertips just brushing mine. Her knees are nudging mine too, as a matter of fact. I can't help feeling a bit silly. I do hope I'm not going to start giggling.

"Let us gaze into the crystal," Madame Rosalie commands.

I gaze obediently. I can't see anything at all. The surface stays milky white and opaque. I glance at Madame Rosalie. She is gazing so hard her eyes look as if they might pop from her head. I try widening my own eyes but I just make them start watering. I blink and wipe them with the back of my hand.

"Do not break the magic circle," says Madame Rosalie.

"Sorry! Er . . . can you see anything in the crystal ball?" I whisper.

"Wait!" says Madame Rosalie.

I wait. I seem to be waiting for ages. Madame Rosalie is still staring terribly intently. I start to get a bit worried. Perhaps she can see something really startlingly dreadful and she doesn't want to alarm me.

I'm feeling very fidgety. I'm not used to kneeling. I'm starting to get dreadful pins and needles. I try to shift my legs very slightly and Madame Rosalie looks up and frowns.

"If you want to commune you must learn to concentrate, dear."

"Yes, I know. It's just I've got these awful pins and needles and—"

"You must learn to rise above such things. Concentrate on your inner soul, not your outer corporeal body. If you wish to master the science of soul culture so that your soul can wander freely upon the astral planes you must meditate. I advise twice daily practice. Half an hour at the very least, morning and evening."

I blink at her. How on earth can I meditate for half an hour when Rachel and Tracy are racketing around me and Craig's yelling and . . . ?

"An hour is even better," Madame Rosalie says firmly. "You will benefit by developing a keener mind, a steadier pulse, brighter eyes, purer thought, a sweet temper, a holier calm, and a gradual cessation of all passionate desires."

I frown. "I'm not sure I really want all that," I say doubtfully. "It might be a bit boring."

"Boring!" says Madame Rosalie. "To step out into the spirit spheres!"

"Is that what you do then? Step out into the spirit world?"

"Well. Not as yet. It takes many years of preparation."

"But I don't want to step out. I want to stop this Victorian girl stepping into me."

"But it's a remarkable blessing to be able to commune with the spirits of the dead. Especially when you're so young and totally untrained. You surely don't want this visitation to cease altogether?"

"Oh yes I do. Please, Madame Rosalie. You've got to help me. What does the crystal ball say?"

"It is all a little hazy at the moment. There are troubled emanations. It's difficult to get a clear reading. Of course, it doesn't help with you keeping on fidgeting and chattering. And maybe the fog in the atmosphere is blocking communication for today."

"But you must be able to see something!"

"It's not like a television set. You don't just switch it on to the right channel," says Madame Rosalie crossly. "I'm doing my best, but it's not clear, I tell you. I can sense there are troubled times ahead for you, dear, but I can't quite understand in what way. It's coming from so far away. It's all faded – like very old photographs. But it's definitely you, dear – well, I can sense it's you, you've got the right psychic aura – and yet it doesn't somehow look like you. This girl's plumper – with curly hair – and she's wearing fancy clothes."

"Maybe it's her, Madame Rosalie! The Victorian girl!" I say excitedly.

I peer desperately at the crystal ball. It stays obstinately opaque.

"Oh, *please*," I say, bending forward until my eyes are inches away from the crystal.

"Not so close," Madame Rosalie warns – but I lean even closer, staring and staring, my eyes watering with the strain.

"Please let me see her too," I whisper fervently to the crystal ball. I stare until everything blurs and I have to blink. I think I see a shadow in the crystal and I lean still further forward.

"*Is there anybody there?*" I whisper.

I blink again. The room seems to have got much darker all of a sudden. I can hardly see anything – not even Madame Rosalie. But the crystal is whiter than ever, its moon glow increasing. There *is* a shadowy figure. I blink again – and see a face. A face, looking back at me. Is it my own face, a ghostly reflection? It seems to be me, it's a girl's face, she's looking anxious, she's blinking, I'm blinking too, it must be me – and yet she *isn't* me.

The room's so dark now, darker than I've ever known before, so dark I can't even see the vague shape of things any more, so profoundly dark that it's almost as if they've been blotted out altogether. I reach out for Madame Rosalie's hand but I can't feel it. I can't find her in this sudden overpowering darkness. I try to call her name but I can't seem to make any sound, even though I'm sure my mouth is open wide. I put my hands up to check – but I can't find my own face in this terrible darkness. I seem to have lost my own shape, my own self!

But the crystal ball is brighter than ever, casting its powerful, pearly glow in the very centre of the darkness. The girl in the crystal is shaking her head, turning this way and that, her mouth open wide in a silent scream. I stare at her and she seems to grow bigger, her head pressing now at the top of the globe, her arms and legs hopelessly cramped. She crouches down like a baby, her head hard against her knees, but she's still growing – I know she's still growing, although my eyes are now squeezed tightly shut and I can't even lift my head to take a proper look. I'm stuck within the darkness and it's hard against me, it hurts so badly, I can't stand it any longer, the pressure, the pain, help me, please help me . . .

What is it? What's happened? There's a splintering, a shattering, my head's bursting right through the crystal, my whole body, my arms and legs, I'm free and spinning in space, whirling round in the darkness, backwards and backwards, hurtled helplessly in this great black void, and it goes on and on and on until I think I shall be spinning backwards for ever, when suddenly there's a jolt, a terrible jarring, and then I bang my head so hard I can scarcely think.

"Miss Victoria? Oh, speak to me, Miss, do. Here, Blanche, have you got them smelling salts? Wave them right under her nose, she's out cold, poor lamb."

I smell something sharply revolting. It vaguely reminds me of Craig's baby nappies. I give a little heave and shudder.

"That's it! She's coming round now. Give her the salts again, Blanche."

"Please don't! What is it? Where am I?"

I open my eyes – and then I close them again, because I simply don't believe what I see. It's a dream. I must have fallen asleep at Madame Rosalie's, yes, that's what happened. I fell asleep while I was staring at that weird crystal ball.

I open my eyes a fraction – and see the crystal ball glowing on the table. I turn to the woman holding my hands, willing her to be dear familiar Madame Rosalie – but it's no use. She's a complete stranger, a very stout woman in a vast white apron. There's another woman too, thin and dark, with a funny cap that's slipped sideways.

"Oh no! Who are you?" I whisper.

"You know me, surely, Miss! I've been in service with your family since you were a babe in arms. You know your old Blanche, don't you? And Mrs Hubbard here. We always lodge with her when we come to Fairhaven. Oh lordie, she looks as if she's never seen us in her life before! Maybe I ought to run for the doctor, Mrs Hubbard?"

"And then what will your Missus say, eh?"

"Oh Miss Victoria, please come to your senses. Don't get us into trouble. Missus doesn't hold with this fortune-telling caper. If she finds out you've been looking at the crystal ball with me and Mrs Hubbard she'll give me my notice, I know she will. She's that worried about you as it is, without you going into a trance. *Miss Victoria!*" Blanche puts her hands on my shoulders and starts gently shaking me. Her hands are very red, with sores at the knuckles.

"What have you done to your hands?" I whisper.

"My hands, Miss? Nothing," she says, looking puzzled.

"But they're all chapped and bleeding."

"That's just all the hard work, the scrubbing and the washing and that."

"Your Missus ought to get in a proper charwoman to do the rough," says the fat woman, Mrs Hubbard. "I have a girl in to help me in the summer months, when I'm extra busy. It's different out of season,

61

of course. I normally close down in November, but when your Missus sent word the young lady here needed a change of air because she'd been poorly, and the little boys would also find the sea breezes beneficial, I opened up my apartments willingly enough, though I don't usually take in invalids."

"Invalids! There's nothing wrong with my young masters and miss – although I won't be able to say as much if we don't go home soon," says Blanche, shivering. "This nasty damp air can't be good for a body. And the wind blows off the sea something wicked. As for this fog, well, you can't tell me that's healthy."

"My house isn't damp," says Mrs Hubbard huffily. "I have a nice coal fire in all my rooms. Your Ma said it was very cosy, didn't she, Miss Victoria?"

"How are you feeling now, Miss?" Blanche asks anxiously. "You're getting a bit of colour in your cheeks. You know who I am really, don't you?"

"You're . . . Blanche," I say tentatively.

"That's right! And who's this?" Blanche says, pointing.

"It's Mrs Hubbard," I say obligingly.

"There!" They beam at each other in obvious relief. Mrs Hubbard bustles to a jar on the kitchen dresser and tips a handful of sultanas on to a saucer. "Here you are, Miss Victoria. Have a little treat. I know you and your brothers help yourselves when my back's turned. It's a wonder there's any sultanas left when I go to make a nice Spotted Dick."

I nibble at the sultanas, which are very sweet, though a little gritty. I peer round the kitchen. I look at the alcove by the window. I've seen it before. It's the alcove in Madame Rosalie's kitchen – where I ate my Sunday lunch an hour ago. I can still smell the

62

delicious roast beef and Yorkshire pudding – and yet Mrs Hubbard has obviously cooked this meal.

"How did I get here?" I whisper.

"You know how we got here, Miss," says Blanche. "We travelled here on the railway yesterday – and my, what a bother that was! Young Master Peterkin screaming his head off the entire journey – I could hear him right back in the third class carriage – and Master George nearly got left behind when he ran up the platform to get a close look at the engine – and then your poor Ma mislaid her portmanteau at the station and there was such a fuss."

"I can imagine!" says Mrs Hubbard.

"She'll make even more of a fuss if she finds out what we've been up to. She blames me for telling Miss Victoria about the seance I attended. It gave Miss Victoria the idea and she played at seances with her friends from school – and then she started having these funny turns. The Missus blames it on the seance lark. She's dead set against anything supernatural, the Missus is. If she knows we've been consulting the crystal ball for Miss Victoria she'll really bust her bodice – pardon the expression, Miss." Blanche nods at me worriedly. "Oh dear, you're still looking so bewildered."

"I can't quite remember what happened," I say artfully. "Can you tell me, Blanche?"

"Well. After we'd done all the lunch dishes Mrs Hubbard here got out her crystal ball – she's got the gift, you know – and we started a little session. It was ever so enjoyable. Mrs Hubbard saw all sorts of things about me and my Henry – you know, Miss, the nice tall constable that takes a cup of tea with me occasionally." Blanche giggles and turns a little pink.

63

"You mean he's your boyfriend?"

"Oh Miss! What an expression. He's my gentleman caller – only not a word to your Ma. Anyways, you came down into the kitchen then, for a bit of company, like, and you joined in the fun and all, asking Mrs Hubbard to consult the crystal on your behalf. It seemed a harmless bit of fun. We never meant to upset you in any way."

"Why? What happened? What did you see, Mrs Hubbard?" I ask.

"I didn't see a thing," says Mrs Hubbard. "The crystal went cloudy."

"But you came over all queer, Miss Victoria," says Blanche. "You kept staring at the crystal as if you could see something really frightening, and then you rocked backwards in your chair and hit your head such a thump on the floor. You just lay there, so white and still, and ooh we had such a fright! We thought you'd passed away on the spot. But then your eyelids started fluttering and you gave these odd little moans and I hoped you were just having another of your funny turns. You are better now, aren't you, Miss? You don't want to get us into trouble, do you?"

I shake my head slowly. My hair bounces on my back. I run my hands through a lot of curls and get my fingers caught up in awful ringlets. I look down at myself. I see an odd fancy woollen frock with long sleeves, a tight bodice and skirts to the tips of my button boots. I stand up and go over to the kitchen dresser. I pick up a gleaming saucepan and peer at myself. Only of course I am no longer myself. It's all happened in reverse. I've gone back into her place. I'm stuck here in the past.

Five

I stand staring into the saucepan, shivering a little.
My reflection stares back at me, slightly distorted by
the gleaming copper. I shut my eyes. She's blotted
out. I open my eyes. She's looking at me. I open my
mouth. She copies me. I mouth the word "Help!"
She silently cries for help too.

I glance up and see Mrs Hubbard and Blanche
eyeing me warily. I replace the saucepan, feeling a
fool.

"I always scrub out my saucepans by hand, Miss.
You'll not find a speck of dirt or rust," Mrs Hubbard
says defensively.

"Oh, I'm sure you do," I say, blushing. "I wasn't
examining it. I was just – just looking at myself."

"Why don't you have a peep in the big looking
glass in the hall, Miss Victoria?" says Blanche.
"You've mussed up all your pretty hair. Better
set yourself to rights. Have you got a lump on
your head from where you bumped it? Let me
have a look." She peers at my hair, gently feeling
my scalp. "I don't *think* there's any lumps or bumps."

"If you want your bumps reading, then I'm the
expert," says Mrs Hubbard. "I can tell a person's
character straight off with just one quick prod of
their cranium."

"You leave her be!" says Blanche. She finishes
examining my head and gives my chin a little chuck
with her poor sore hands. "There! You're all right
now, aren't you, Miss Victoria?"

"I suppose so," I say. It's no use trying to tell

them what really happened. I know they'll think me even odder than I am. And how can I explain it all when I don't understand it myself?

"You won't breathe a word to your Ma, eh?" says Blanche. "It would be more than my job's worth, I'm telling you."

"No, all right. I promise. Only . . . *why* would she give you the sack if she found out?"

"Beg pardon, Miss?"

"Why would she make you leave?"

"Well, she doesn't think it decent and God-fearing, trying to tell what's in store for us. I've tried to explain it's just a bit of harmless fun but it's no use. Your Ma caught me reading young Nellie's palm the other day and she nearly split her stays – pardon the expression, Miss."

"Will you read my palm, Blanche?" I say, holding my hand out.

"Oh no, Miss!"

"I'll take a look, Miss Victoria," says Mrs Hubbard. "Palm-reading's another one of my specialities."

"I said no, Mrs Hubbard," says Blanche, but Mrs Hubbard is already peering at my palm with great interest.

"Well, I never did!" she exclaims.

"You mustn't frighten Miss Victoria," Blanche warns worriedly.

"It's not bad news, Blanche," says Mrs Hubbard. "Miss Victoria's got no call to feel frightened."

"So it's good news, is it?" I ask hopefully. "A change of scenery in the near future, perhaps? Or the distant future might be even better!"

"I don't know about that. It's your life-line, Miss. You've got two of them! A double line, running right across your palm. I haven't seen nothing like it in all my born days."

"I might have known," I say, sighing. "Tell me more, Mrs Hubbard."

A bell rings suddenly.

"Not now, Miss. That's your Ma in my guest drawing room, wanting her tea. You'd better run and join her," says Mrs Hubbard.

Blanche straightens her cap and smooths her apron, and then starts setting a tea tray. Mrs Hubbard bustles to the kettle singing on the range. She creaks as she walks. I'm not sure whether it's her boots or her corsets.

"Not a word to your Ma, Miss," Blanche says again, tinkling teacups.

"Not a word, I promise," I say uncomfortably. I hesitate. "Blanche. Do you – do you mind having to do whatever my Mum – my Mamma tells you?"

"Mind, Miss?"

"Well, it just seems so unfair. Why should you have to flap round just because she rings a bell? And why on earth can't you tell fortunes or do whatever you like? She's got no right to tell you two what to do."

They're both looking shocked.

"And you've got no right to talk about your Ma in that way," says Mrs Hubbard. "I've never heard the like! And only yesterday you acted like butter wouldn't melt in your mouth, quite the little lady."

"She's growing up a bit," says Blanche, giving me a pat. "Turning into one of these modern girls who want to set the world to rights. She'll be campaigning for voting rights soon."

"I'm much more modern than you think, Blanche," I say.

"Well, run along anyway, Miss. We've got our work to do now, whether you like it or we like it."

It's very hard to run along when you haven't got a clue where you're going. I find my way out of the basement by going up the stairs. I'm in a strange draughty hall with a big mirror. I take another look at myself. It's still such a shock that I stand transfixed. I can't stand the way I look. It isn't just the periwinkle blue dress – and whatever else I've got on underneath. (It feels like steel plating and it's practically cutting me in two, and I think I've got weird old-lady knickers on as well, because there's something baggy flapping right down past my knees.) It's my awful hairstyle, prinked here, puffed up there, with the *ringlets*. I look such a prize berk. And my face is such a terrible twitty face too, all long lashes and plump pink cheeks and pert little mouth. I don't look *real*.

I pull terrible gargoyle faces at myself to stop looking like a china doll.

"Victoria! Whatever are you doing, child?"

My features shoot back into place. I turn round, gulping. There's a woman standing in the doorway. She's obviously my mamma. Oh help. She looks *awful*. She's got my hairstyle too, only it's looped up more at the back, and the fringe is all fussy little curly bits. She's got the same dumb doll face as me, although she's got little lines everywhere as if her china's cracking. She's wearing the most amazing brown velvet dress trimmed with gold tassles, that makes her look like an overstuffed sofa. She's got two bracelets on one plump wrist, three bangles on the other, rings on every finger, a big brooch at the neck, and a watch on a long gold chain. She looks as if she'll start chiming when she walks. She smells strongly of violets.

I approach her warily. The violets become over-powering. I'd much sooner the soapy sweaty smell of Blanche and Mrs Hubbard in the kitchen.

"Victoria? Why were you grimacing in such an extraordinary fashion? Oh dear, you weren't having another seizure, were you?"

"No, Mamma." I want to burst out laughing, it sounds so funny. And yet what else can I do but play along with this? After all, it isn't as if I'm stuck here forever. I always wake up as myself when Victoria takes me over in my time. So I've just got to string along with this Victorian lark till bedtime and then tomorrow morning I'll wake up as me. I wonder if I'll remember it all? Old Mr Maxfield, my History teacher, won't half be impressed by my first-hand account of Victorian times!

I look about me as I follow Mamma into what must be the drawing room. It's like walking into an antique shop – only the colours are all so bright and it all looks brand new. I walk round the room in a daze, trying to take it all in. There's so many bits and pieces everywhere, tiny tables, funny screens, ornaments crammed in every nook and cranny, little stools – it's an obstacle race getting from one side of the room to the other.

"I can't get used to this room either," says the Mamma, as if she's reading my thoughts. "It's all so dreary and old-fashioned. These seaside lodgings are all the same. Still, I'd sooner come to Mrs Hubbard's than try a hotel again. Those people at the Royal were particularly offensive last year, daring to complain about Peterkin. Is he still taking his nap, Victoria? And what about Georgie? Run upstairs and see what Nellie's doing. I'm not sure that girl will prove satisfactory. Maybe I should have kept Lizzie after all. At least she knew her place even if she couldn't keep the boys under control. What do you think, my pet?"

The pet doesn't know what to say. She talks about real people as if they're dresses in her wardrobe and she can throw them out if she feels they don't suit her.

"Don't gawp at me like that, Victoria! And whilst you're upstairs, do attend to your hair. Did you brush it when you took off your bonnet when we came home from church? No, I think not!" Mamma waves me away with her bejewelled fingers.

I find myself back in the hall. I go up the staircase to the first floor. I peer into a big bedroom that is obviously Mamma's, with large ornate dresses like lampshades hanging up all round the room and a clutter of jewellery on the dressing table. There's a great big bed with fancy brass bedposts and a white coverlet – but it doesn't hang right down to the carpet. I can see a rose-patterned chamber pot under the bed. I imagine Mamma in her nightgown plumping herself down on the pot and I start spluttering hysterically.

There's a pretty silver hairbrush on the dressing table and I stab at my ringlets without much success. I haven't got a clue how they're meant to go. Oh well, it's just too bad.

I go back to the stairs and try the next floor. I pause on the landing. I can hear something. Little soft sniffly sounds. Someone's crying. Peterkin?

I open the door and peer round. It's a much smaller, plainer room, without ornament. Someone is sitting sobbing on the narrow bed. But it's not a

70

little brother Peterkin. It's a girl about my own age, in a rather grubby apron and a print frock. She must be another servant. Nellie the nursery maid. But she's not a big grown woman like Blanche. She's only about my age, or even younger. She seems much smaller than me as she hunches on the bed, her head in her hands. She gives a desolate sniff and then wipes her nose with the back of her hand. It still stays very damp. I've got a crisp white lace handkerchief sticking out of my velvet trimmed cuff.

"Here. Have a blow on this," I say, offering her the hankie.

She jumps violently.

"What's up? You're not scared of me, are you?"

"I'm scared of you getting me into trouble," she says fiercely.

"No, I won't, I promise."

"Anyways, you can't get me into trouble because I haven't done nothing today," she says, sniffing again.

She ignores my proffered hankie, lifts up her skirt, and dabs at her nose with a corner of her petticoat. I thought Victorians were so modest they even draped the legs of their pianos! This girl is exposing a lot of her black holey stockings without turning a hair. She's obviously a servant but she's certainly not behaving in a subservient way.

"You're spying on me, aren't you, Miss," she says indignantly.

"Me, spy? Come off it! I just came to tell George and Peterkin that tea is nearly ready."

"Well, why don't you go to *their* room then? Why come nosing in here?"

"I heard you crying."

"I was doing it quietly!"

71

"But what's the matter?" I remember a sad sob-story I once read about a little Victorian servant girl starving in an attic.

"Are you hungry, Nellie? Here, let me get you something to eat."

"I've had two helpings of that Mrs Hubbard's Yorkshire pudding at dinner," she says. "I'm full to bursting."

"Oh. Well. Are you warm enough?"

"I've been carrying on so that I've got myself in a right lather," she says, feeling her scarlet cheeks.

"So why are you crying then?"

"What's it to you, Miss?"

"I don't know. I'm just trying to be friendly."

"Friendly?" she says suspiciously. "A fine friend you were yesterday, Miss – telling tales on me to your mamma because you saw me give Peterkin a little shake."

"Well, that was yesterday," I say quickly. "Sorry about that. I bet you'll find I'm very different now. And I don't care if you shake little Peterkin until he rattles. I still won't tell."

She stares at me, sniffing. I offer the handkerchief again and this time she takes it and gives her nose a proper blow.

"Thank you, Miss. Shall I wash it out for you?"

"No, you keep it."

"How can I do that? I can't wave a bit of dainty lace about every time I sniffle. What would your mamma say? She'd think I'd stolen it."

"I'll tell her I've given it to you as a present."

"She'd think you'd gone off your head then," says Nellie tartly. "You don't give presents to servants except at Christmas – and even then it's only material for new uniforms."

"Really? I hate the way things are now. No wonder you were crying."

"Blubbing like a baby," she says. "I should be ashamed of myself. But I was just that downhearted I couldn't help myself. This is supposed to be my Sunday off, Miss, remember? Only how can I go and see Mother and all my brothers and sisters without the fare from Fairhaven? It's that unfair. I only get the one Sunday a month and I look forward to it so badly."

"How do you get home normally? Is it near us?"

"Quite near. I have to walk the six miles there and the six miles back, which isn't so grand because my boots nip my toes something chronic – but it isn't half worth it when I get there. Mother and the little ones give me such a welcome. But if I tried to walk home from Fairhaven I'd be walking all day and night and I'd still never get more than halfway."

"But that's so mean! Couldn't you explain and ask my mamma for the fare?" I suggest – but my voice wavers as I see Nellie's scornful expression. "Oh dear. I suppose there's no point trying. And it's sort of my fault you're stuck here," I say guiltily. "Because of my . . . my funny turns."

"You seem to have taken a mighty funny turn this afternoon, Miss Victoria," says Nellie – but she's smiling. "You've been such a hoity-toity pious petal up until today, hardly deigning to look in my direction, and yet now we've been chatting away quite the thing."

"I wish we could stay this way," I say. "I'm afraid tomorrow I'll probably go back to being a snotty old bossyboots."

Nellie snorts with laughter and puts her hand over her mouth to stop her splutters.

"Come, Miss. I'd better see to the boys. Peterkin will have woken from his nap by now – and heaven knows what Georgie's up to."

I follow her down one flight of stairs and on to the landing. Nellie rushes past the bedroom occupied by Mamma, negotiates a little passage, and then opens another door. It's obviously the boys' room. There are two iron beds, two bedside tables, two wardrobes – but no sign of the two boys, though Nellie peers under the beds and inside the wardrobes.

"They're playing some trick on me," she says. She cocks her head. "Did you hear giggles, Miss? Oh dear, I think they've got into your bedroom."

We go further down the passage. The giggles are getting louder.

"Whatever are you up to, you naughty boys?" Nellie demands, opening the door on them. Then she gives a gasp.

I peer over her shoulder. I blink. Where are the two boys? I can only see two odd little girls – a big one with short brown curly hair and a little one with a head of ringlets to rival my own. They are dressed in awful fancy frocks, one pink, one lilac, with such long skirts they've tucked them right up into their huge baggy bloomers.

"George! Peterkin! How *dare* you dress up in Miss Victoria's best frocks," Nellie says, rushing at them. "Oh, you bad, bad boys, you've got them all crushed. Peterkin, look, you've split the sleeve! Oh Miss Victoria, I'm that sorry."

She turns to me, looking aghast. Even the boys look a little frightened. I stare at them – and burst out laughing.

"What a pair of little cissies they look, Nellie," I say. "We ought to make them dress like that all the time just to punish them. I bet all their friends wouldn't half laugh at them."

"No, they wouldn't!" says George, the bigger one, pulling his frock over his head quickly.

"Get mine off too!" says Peterkin, tugging.

"Careful! Don't you dare tear it any more," says Nellie, trying to rescue the dresses.

She handles the delicate material very carefully, stroking it reverently with her rough little hands. I look at Nellie's old print frock, the coarse grey material, the patches at the elbows, the line at the bottom to show the hem's been let down. I'd give anything for Nellie to have the fancy dresses instead of me.

"I'm really going to be for it now," Nellie sighs as she hustles the boys into their own clothes.

"It's not *your* fault, Nellie," I say indignantly. "Look, we can sew up that sleeve easily enough."

"But Peterkin's got boot marks on the skirt!"

"I'm sure they'll wash off – or we can send it to the dry-cleaners," I say.

"Send it where, Miss?"

"Oh! It doesn't matter that much anyway. Personally I think they're hideous, both of them."

"Oh Miss! They're beautiful. And you two boys are so wicked you ought to be whipped," says Nellie, giving both of them a little shake.

"Mamma says you mustn't touch us, Nellie," says George smugly.

"No, Mamma will whip *you* if you shake or slap us," Peterkin pipes up.

"Listen, you two," I say. "You're both horrible little pigs. Don't you dare touch any of my stuff again. And don't be so cheeky to Nellie either, you silly little twits."

75

They back away from me, looking amazed. But then Georgie stands his ground.

"You can't do anything. You're only a girl," he says stoutly.

"Oh yeah?" I say – and I suddenly leap forward, get him in a headlock and wrestle him swiftly to the carpet. All those Saturday afternoons watching dear old Big Daddy wrestling on the telly have turned up trumps at last!

"Help! Mercy!" Georgie rasps.

"Okay. But only if you behave yourself in future. And you, Peter-Pigkin. *Or else!*" I say grandly, releasing the squirming George. "I don't think you'll have any more trouble out of them today, anyway," I say to Nellie.

"I think you'll have to give me fighting lessons, Miss Victoria," says Nellie, grinning. "Well, I never did."

I skip triumphantly down the stairs – but I'm put severely in my place by my fussy finnicky Mamma, who is wondering where on earth we've all got to. She gives George and Peterkin a lecture too, asking them where they've been and why Nellie hasn't sent them sooner.

"It wasn't Nellie's fault," I say quickly. "Was it, George?"

"Certainly not," says George hastily.

"I want my cake!" says Peterkin, grabbing at the plate on the side-table.

"Careful, my darling," says Mamma. "Here, precious. Let Mamma help you."

Peterkin gets his pick of all the cakes – and then George. I have to wait my turn, which seems ever so unfair seeing as I'm older than both of them.

"Why do I come last, Mamma?" I ask.

76

Mamma looks surprised. "Well, dear. You are the girl. We must always attend to your brothers first."

"*Why?*" I say indignantly.

"Because boys are better than girls, that's why," says George, his mouth full of cake.

"What rubbish!" I say.

"Boys are much better," says Peterkin.

"Well, you can shut up for a start, because you're just a baby," I say to squash him.

"Victoria! Please don't take that tone with your brothers. Really! What unladylike behaviour. Whatever has got into you today, my dear? You're not yourself at all."

"You're telling me," I mutter.

After we've had tea and poor Blanche has cleared away all the dishes, Mamma suggests I read aloud to the two boys from some terrible turgid annual called *Sunday Smiles*.

"Can't I read from a proper story book?" I ask. "This looks awfully boring."

"Victoria! Do stop being so difficult. Story books aren't suitable for Sunday reading. Now. Please read one of the nice tales in *Sunday Smiles*."

I try. I start this amazingly awful account of some pert little girl who gives her silver sixpence to a draggled beggar on the streets who is so grateful he kisses the hem of her frock. I can't help making mock vomit noises at this point. The boys appreciate my performance enormously but Mamma is furious.

"Victoria! How dare you behave in such a disgraceful manner! You will go to bed at once, do you hear me?"

I hear her. I don't care a bit. In fact I can't wait

to go to bed. The sooner I get to sleep the better. I can't stick being stuck in the past. I can't wait to get back to my own time.

Six

I wake up – and remember everything immediately. Imagine being wafted right back to Victorian times! It was all so incredibly vivid too.

"Here, Tracy, Rachel! Wake up, you two! You'll never guess what happened to me yesterday," I say, sitting up and rubbing my eyes.

I look over at their beds. And then I rub my eyes again and again, desperately pressing against the lids. I try again. Oh no, what am I going to do? I haven't gone back. I'm not in my own bedroom with Tracy and Rachel. I'm still stuck here in the past.

It *can't* be true! Always before when Victoria switched places with me everything righted itself overnight. Perhaps it isn't morning yet?

I rush to the curtains and tear them aside. It *is* morning. Yesterday's fog has cleared. The sky is blue, the sun is already out. The trees are all shades of red and gold. It's a beautiful autumn day. For a moment things look so normal that I can't believe it. A man in a bowler hat and a formal suit walks briskly along the road. He doesn't look *that* different. But then two women cross the road, carrying big baskets. They're wearing trimmed straw hats with big shawls and long skirts. They have to waddle hurriedly out the way of a horse and cart. A scruffy little boy in a cap and breeches to his knees imitates their waddle behind their backs. It's real. It's not a dream, it's not a film set. I'm truly back in the past. What am I going to do? How on earth am I ever going to get back to my own time?

A seagull flies past the window, mewing mockingly. I lean my forehead against the cold window pane, tears welling up in my eyes. What's happening a hundred years in the future? If only there was some way of getting in touch with Mum and telling her where I am. What happened after Tracy's football match? How would she ever find me at Madame Rosalie's house? And if she even found the house, what would Madame Rosalie say? Oh, sorry dearie, but your sister's just popped back into the past, travelling via the crystal ball, and I'm afraid I don't know if she's got a return ticket or not.

The crystal ball! That's it. That's how it happened. Madame Rosalie consulted her crystal ball – and a hundred years ago exactly Mrs Hubbard consulted her crystal too. Victoria and I might even have been in the very same spot – and I got materialized back into her. So the only way back to being me in the present is via the crystal ball!

I run out of my room and race downstairs, nearly tripping headlong over my trailing Victorian nightgown. I hitch it up around my knees and carry on running. I find the door in the main hall leading down to Mrs Hubbard's kitchen. She's up already, bustling about at the kitchen range, stirring a large pot of porridge.

"Oh my! You gave me a fright, Miss Victoria," she says, hands to her great shelf of bosom. "My heart! What's the matter, Miss? Have you been took bad?"

"I'm all right. No, I'm not. Oh, Mrs Hubbard, please help me," I say desperately. "Where's your crystal ball?"

80

"What, now, Miss? I'm in the middle of making my porridge. If your Ma's really against consulting the crystal then I shouldn't let you, especially as it gave you such a nasty turn yesterday."

"But that's why I need to look into it now. To make me better again. Oh *please*, Mrs Hubbard."

"Right you are, Miss. There's no need to work yourself up into a state. Watch that porridge then. A few spoonfuls of my porridge, with cream fresh from the farm, and you'll soon stop all these nervous turns, dearie." She goes to the kitchen dresser, clambers precariously on a stool, and reaches into a great willow-patterned tureen right on the top shelf. She brings out a red velvet cloth wrapped about a globe shape.

"It's just the same as Madame Rosalie's," I say excitedly.

"Who's this Madame Rosalie then? You've not been going to one of them gypsy fortune-tellers, have you? You keep away from the likes of them, Miss. Here! Give that porridge a stir, it's sticking!"

I give it a hasty stir and then rush to Mrs Hubbard as she unwraps the crystal and sets it carefully on the kitchen table. I peer desperately at the crystal ball.

"It's all misty!" I wail. "Can you see anything, Mrs Hubbard?"

"I'm not sure, Miss. Hush a minute. Let me concentrate."

I hush with difficulty. I hold my breath, trying so hard to remember exactly what happened with Madame Rosalie. Did I do anything in particular to trigger the timeswitch mechanism? Did I say anything? I rack my brains frantically. I think I asked Madame Rosalie a specific question. If I could only

81

repeat the exact words then it might all happen in reverse – and I could get back.

I took a deep breath.

"Is there . . . ?"

I feel a slight shift sideways, a tingling down my spine. I think I'm nearly there. I've almost got it.

"Is there . . . a girl in the crystal?" I try.

It's not quite right. Nothing happens. But Mrs Hubbard is leaning forward, very close to the crystal ball.

"A girl, Miss? Yes. Yes, I think there is," she says, though her voice sounds uncertain.

"What sort of a girl? What does she look like?"

"It's hard to make out, Miss."

"Please try, Mrs Hubbard. It's so important. This girl. Is she about my age – but with different clothes? You'll think they look odd. Like boy's clothes. Her hair will be tied back any old how. Can you see a girl like that?"

"Is she a friend of yours, Miss? She doesn't sound like a young lady, if you ask me. Boy's clothes, you say?"

"Yes. Oh please. Can you see her? Is there . . . is there any . . . any sign of her?" I peer close to the crystal, trying so hard to see her for myself.

"Try not to breathe on the crystal, Miss, you'll make it even mistier."

"The girl, Mrs Hubbard."

"I can't be sure, Miss. It's just a shape."

"Can't you try to make her into the right shape?"

"You can't exert your own will on what the crystal shows. We have no influence over the future, we just have to take what comes."

"But I don't want to take it, I want to change it," I insist.

"What's this I see now?" says Mrs Hubbard. She gives a little suspicious sniff. "I smell trouble!"

"And I smell something burning!" says a sharp voice behind us.

Blanche is standing in the door of the kitchen, her hands on her hips.

"Whatever are you two up to?" she demands.

"My porridge!" Mrs Hubbard wails, leaping up. Her arms fly outwards and she catches the crystal with the back of her hand. It tips off the edge of the table and smashes onto the hard tiled floor.

"Oh no!"

The three of us stare at the shattered glass.

"My crystal ball!" Mrs Hubbard shrieks. "And my porridge is burned too. It's all your fault, Miss Victoria. You didn't ought to have come bothering me."

"I'm sorry," I say, and then I burst into tears because it looks as if my hopes of getting back to the present are shattered as surely as the crystal.

"There now, Miss! Don't take on so," says Blanche, and she puts her arms round me. "Mind your bare feet with all that nasty glass about. Come on, now. Stop your crying. You've said you're sorry to poor Mrs Hubbard. Don't take on so. It's not the end of the world."

But it does seem to be the end of my world. I can't stop crying, no matter how hard I try. Blanche rocks me against her warm starchy apron, her rough hands gently patting my back.

"Come on now, little Miss," says Mrs Hubbard. "I daresay I can make another pot of porridge easy enough. It's not the first one that's burnt and it won't be the last."

"But the crystal ball. It's broken!" I sob. "I'll ask Mamma to give you the money for another one."

"Don't do that, Miss!" says Blanche quickly.

"Wouldn't be no use anyways. You can't go out and buy a crystal ball like a pound of best butter," says Mrs Hubbard, starting to clear up all the shattered pieces with a dustpan and brush. "My old Auntie passed this one on to me, seeing as I had the gift. Lord knows where she got it from. And Lord knows where I'll ever get another."

"Oh Mrs Hubbard, I'm so sorry. I feel so awful. I know I shouldn't have bothered you. But I was just so desperate to see into the crystal – and now I've ruined everything."

"There now," says Mrs Hubbard, popping a handful of sultanas into my mouth. "Calm yourself down, ducks. It was me that knocked the crystal flying after all. I'd better scrape the pot and start on another stir of porridge or we'll all go hungry this morning."

"And you'd better run upstairs and get yourself washed and dressed, Miss," says Blanche. "I never heard the like. Wandering round the house without even a shawl round you. You'll catch your death. Look at you, you've shivering."

But I'm shivering with shock rather than cold. I'd pinned all my hopes on the crystal ball and now I don't know what I'm going to do. Am I going to be stuck here for ever and ever? And no matter how old I grow I'll never be able to catch up with my own times. I'll be in my forties by the end of the First World War, an old age pensioner during the Second. If I even make it into the Swinging Sixties I'll be an ancient old crone – and I'll be long dead and buried by the time the real me is thirteen in her present.

I don't even know *how* to get washed and dressed. I look in vain for a bathroom before realizing that the jug of tepid water Blanche has put in my room is my only means of washing. And getting my underwear on is a nightmare. I try to jettison the corset but then I don't fit into my dresses properly. My boots are another trial. I fiddle with the stiff little buttons, break two nails, and get nowhere.

I hobble along the corridor to the boys' room, where Nellie is slapping George and Peterkin into their clothes. They are both giggling and dancing about and singing what they obviously think is an uproariously rude song. It has a single line of lyrics: "Our Nellie has a Belly".

"Beg Pardon, Miss," says Nellie, scarlet-faced.

"Stop being mean to poor Nellie, you two, or I'll bash you up," I threaten.

"We said belly," Peterkin splutters, still expecting me to be shocked.

"That's nothing. I know far worse words than that," I say airily. "Nellie. I've got stuck with my boots. I know it's stupid, but how do I . . . ?"

"Have you lost your button-hook, Miss?" she says, and she plants Peterkin's foot in a pearl grey boot and starts niftily hooking each button into place with a little curly-headed instrument. "Do you want to borrow this one, Miss?"

I borrow it and soon get the hang of it. My hair is still a problem. I brush it hard and then try to loop parts of it up on top – without success. I hear the boys go galloping downstairs. Nellie pauses in my doorway.

"Here. Let me," she says, coming over and

taking the hairbrush. "Why can't you fix your hair right this morning, eh?"

"I just don't seem to have the knack to do anything right today. It's as if my hands belong to someone else altogether," I say carefully. 'Oh Nellie, I do like the way you're doing it. It's *much* better than those awful ringlets."

"Yes, I've always thought they made you look a bit of a fright," says Nellie. "There! You'll be pinning it all up soon, quite the young lady."

"You've got yours pinned right up – and yet I bet you're not any older than I am."

"Yes, but I'm not a lady, am I," says Nellie, putting in a final pin. "Mind you, with a bit of luck I reckon I could make a lady's maid some day. If I learnt to bow and scrape a bit, and talk more posh."

"Is that what you'd really like to be?"

Nellie wrinkles her nose. "Not really. I don't like being in service. No, what I'd *really* like . . . is to be a typewriter."

"A . . . typewriter?" I say, spluttering a little.

"Yes, Miss, I know it's just a silly pipedream, so of course you find it comical," Nellie says huffily.

"No, it's not that! It's just it sounds so funny. I mean, a typewriter is the actual machine you write your letters on."

"Have you ever seen one? It sounds the most wonderful invention. That's what I'd give anything to do. I'd like to be a typewriter in an elegant office and be treated like a young lady," says Nellie, her eyes shining.

"Maybe you'll get to be a typist one day," I say. "I've got a feeling it might be possible."

I join Mamma and my two new brothers for breakfast. Blanche serves us, which seems ridiculous.

Mrs Hubbard has made another pot of porridge and it tastes truly delicious. Then there's a boiled egg with buttered bread. I've never had such a wonderful meal! The egg is so full of flavour, the butter's really creamy, and the bread is soft inside with a wonderfully crispy crust.

"I'm glad to see your appetite's improved, Victoria," says Mamma. "And you start your water cure treatment with Dr Beamish today."

"Oh dear. Do I have to?" I say worriedly. What on earth is a water cure? Something similar to water torture?

"Don't be so silly, Victoria. That is the whole point of our Fairhaven visit. Now, we are not due at the Hydropathic until eleven so I suggest a stroll along the promenade first. Let us get ready."

It takes ages to get ready to go out. I find my visit to the lavatory very interesting. The bowl has got a willow pattern and you pull a little handle beside the wooden seat. I get dressed up in my outdoor clothes after artfully asking Mamma what she'd like me to wear.

"I think your blue pelisse trimmed with squirrel fur," she suggests.

I pull a horrified face. "Squirrel fur! How dreadful. Oh, the poor things."

Mamma looks at me as if I'm quite mad. She is obviously no animal lover. She seems to have half a bird incorporated into her hideous hat. To my relief my own hat is trimmed with blue velvet roses. I was imagining sad little stuffed squirrel heads.

Nellie has got the boys ready in their reefer coats. They are jumping up and down, eager to see the fishing boats and the fishermen. When we go out they run on ahead, whooping and laughing. I have to walk sedately beside Mamma. Girls obviously aren't expected to whoop and laugh, let alone run. Nellie walks behind us. I turn round to chat to her, but Mamma gives my arm a little pull and frowns at me. I feel so sorry for Nellie, trudging after us in her shabby boots that are too small.

But when we reach the fishing huts Nellie gets to go on the beach with the boys. George and Peterkin rush up to the fishermen mending their nets. They look incredible in their souwesters and smocks, their faces suntanned golden brown even though the summer's long gone. One of the young handsome fishermen starts chatting to Nellie, pretending to throw his fishing net over her. She runs away squealing, her shabby skirt flying up in the air. She's the one having fun now. I'm the one who's left out, stuck mincing along with Mamma.

There are lots of people parading about even though it's November, and there's a band playing merrily in the bandstand. Fairhaven is obviously a favourite spot for the ailing. I see lots of old ladies being wheeled along in bath chairs like giant prams. There's not much to do except parade up and down. There's no amusement arcades along the front. I peer in one of the gift shops.

"Come along, dear. You're not interested in any of that gimcrack rubbish," says Mamma.

She'd be amazed the price those funny ornaments and pieces of pottery would fetch in the antique shops of the present! There aren't any Whippy ice cream stalls of course, but there's a cart standing at the top of the beach, advertising ice cream at a penny a glass.

"Can I try some ice cream please, Mamma?"

I ask as politely as I can, but Mamma gives an affected shudder and refuses.

We're coming up to the pier now and I suddenly hold my breath and pray, hoping against hope to see Madame Rosalie's fortune-telling booth. There's a seafood stall with a man the spitting image of my winkle man – but no sign of any fortune-teller.

But there is a wonderful looking gypsy girl with an embroidered scarf and bolero and a long scarlet skirt standing next to a bird cage. I strain my eyes, reading the sign above the cage. It tells me that these charming birds will pick out a ball to tell "your past and future life".

"Oh Mamma! Have you got a penny? Oh, I must have a go!"

"Don't be so silly, dear. We're not wasting a penny on such foolishness." But Mamma's voice is distracted. She's looking at a pompous little man in a bowler hat who is setting up a giant tripod on the sands. A courting couple are sitting up very straight on stools in front of him, grimacing rigidly.

"I wonder," says Mamma, wavering. "Shall we pose for a tintype portrait, Victoria? It would be a lovely surprise to send to Papa. Only, of course, it seems so vulgar to pose in the open air for all the world to see. Still, we are at the seaside. Things are a little different here."

So we queue up to get our photographs taken. Mamma calls the boys over and commands Nellie to smarm down their hair and pull up their socks. Nellie doesn't get to be in the photograph but she doesn't look as if she cares. She wanders over to the ice cream stall and starts chatting to the old lady, who gives her a free lick.

The photographer arranges Mamma on one stool,

me on another. He places little Peterkin on Mamma's lap, and makes George stand beside me, an arm round my neck.

"Now you must keep very still indeed," he announces.

Peterkin promptly struggles and squirms and kicks and George slyly pinches my neck and makes me jump.

"No, no. Please settle yourselves and try to remain still," says the photographer.

The autumn sun shines surprisingly strongly, making me screw up my eyes.

"Don't squint, Victoria," Mamma commands. "George, stand up straight. And Peterkin dear, do try not to wriggle so."

"The sun's in my eyes, Mamma," Peterkin wails, rubbing them. "I want to go and play."

"In a moment, my lambkin. Just try to be a good boy and stay still for one second. Look at the nice man and smile. And you, George. Victoria dear, set your little brothers an example."

George pinches me again and I yelp.

"Do that once more and I'll stick you in the sand head first," I mutter, staring fixedly at the camera.

The sun is making my eyes water. Rainbow lights sparkle at the corners of my eyes. I try to stare at the glass lens of the camera while a tear dribbles down my cheek.

"I will call my assistant, Ma'am. He will provide you with a sunshade," says the photographer. He clears his throat and shouts over to a wooden hut on wheels decorated with his miniature tinplate photographs. "Boy! Assistance required. Look lively! *Is there anybody there?*"

There's a sudden strange flash. Has he taken

the photo already? I can't see a thing. The light sears my eyes, rainbows sparkle inside my head, I'm tipped up off the stall but I don't land on the sand, I fall through it, tumbling forwards in the flashing light until I suddenly stop with a jolt.

I'm lying flat on my face. I try to lift my head and see weird pink swirls. I blink and they become part of a carpet. Madame Rosalie's carpet!

"I'm back!" I say.

"Oh thank goodness, dearie!" says Madame Rosalie, who is squatting anxiously beside me. "I was starting to get so worried. I've never seen anyone enter a trance instantaneously. And such a profound trance too. I couldn't communicate with you at all. I was beginning to fear you might have passed over to the other side altogether."

"No wonder," I say, sitting up and stretching. "I've been here all night, haven't I? I was so scared when I woke up over there and realized I was stuck."

"Pardon, dearie?" says Madame Rosalie. "You've not been here all night! No, no, you've been out a few minutes at the most."

"So their time isn't the same as our time," I say slowly. "I suppose because it's the past and therefore it's already happened it's like dream time. Anyway, thank goodness I woke up before I got carted off to that Hydropathic place and she's now her and I'm me."

"I think you'd better have a nice cup of tea," says Madame Rosalie. "You're not quite yourself at the moment."

"You bet I am, Madame Rosalie! I'm fine now, really. And I'd better get cracking or I'll miss my sister's football match."

"But you need my help, child."

"I know you did your best, Madame Rosalie, but I don't want to be helped any more. I nearly got stuck in the past, gazing into your crystal. I'd sooner leave things the way they are. I can just about put up with Victoria taking me over in the present. I can't *stand* me going back to being her in the past. So thanks very much for the lovely lunch and the special consultation and all that, but I'll be on my way now."

"You can't walk away from your phenomenal psychic powers, dear. I can guide you, give you special occult instruction. I could use you as a medium in my private seances for the rich and famous. Oh child, if we can only unleash the full potential of your psychic powers then who knows what spiritual secrets we will stumble upon."

"I don't want my psychic powers unleashed any more, Madame Rosalie. I want to chain them up for good. I must go now."

I back away from her pink bedroom and let myself out of her front door. The fog has cleared a little. There's a silvery gleam at the edge of the clouds, as if the sun is trying to get through. I take in great gulps of air and then start sprinting through the town. The match will have started already. Still, I ought to get there before it finishes so I can give Tracy a cheer or two. And Sue. But catch me supporting Amazon Ann. I hope she stays shivering on the sidelines. That two-timing silly little Squirt! And he was positively flaunting this footballing floozie, revelling in the situation. Does he think we're going to trot round in a threesome – Loverboy and Little and Large? Or is he turned on by the thought that Ann and I might start fighting over him? He's was-ting his time. There's no point waging war with an

Amazon. Especially as I'm severely out of shape at the moment. I've only been running two minutes and I'm gasping for breath already – *and* I've got hiccups. You can't eat an old-fashioned Sunday roast and lurch backwards and forwards through a hundred years without getting severe indigestion.

I've still got Tracy's change so I stagger into a sweetshop and buy myself some peppermints. I peer round the shop approvingly at the gaudy bars of chocolate, the video stand, the girlie magazines, the fat blockbuster novels. It all looks so gloriously modern. I still feel a bit shaky when I realize how close I was to getting stuck in the past forever. And I *still* don't see how the timeshift mechanism works.

One of the blockbuster titles catches my eye. "*Petticoat Passion*: the steamy story of a Victorian nubile nursery maid." I pick it up and leaf through this total garbage, snorting. There's a picture of the naughty nubile nincompoop on the cover and they haven't even got her clothes right. She's got a silly little Miss Muffet mop cap on her head, and her bare chest is bursting right out of her bodice. I think of Nellie and the sort of life she led. I could tell what it was *really* like. So why don't I? I always get good marks for soppy school essays. Yes, maybe I'll stop being a psychic phenomenon and start being a writing whizz-kid instead. I could write my own Victorian blockbuster. I wouldn't have to do any boring old research. I can just close my eyes and remember everything – the houses, the clothes, the way people talked, the things they did at the seaside. Maybe I'll make my fortune!

I saunter out of the shop, sucking my peppermint, my eyes half closed as I start composing the first chapter in my head. And then I bump into some boy who's hurtling along the road with his head down—

"Vicky!"

"Squirt!"

"I've been looking *everywhere* for you."

"Why?"

"Because you've been missing for ages and your sister's just about doing her nut because she thinks you might be having another of your funny turns and it's affected her game and so my sister's playing instead and she's doing really well which is really miffing your sister, obviously, but I couldn't concentrate on the match and cheer my sister just in case there was something really wrong with you so I've been looking for you all over and – and that's about it, really," says Squirt breathlessly.

I blink at him.

"Did you say *your* sister?" I say, not sure I caught his drift in this deluge of information.

"Yeah. My sister Ann," says Squirt, grinning. "Only you seemed to jump to crazy conclusions about her, didn't you?"

I am momentarily silenced. I stare at Squirt. And then I smile.

"I seem to have made a bit of a berk of myself," I admit. "So she's your sister, eh? I didn't even know you had a sister. She's not a bit like you, Squirt."

"How about calling me Jack? And I know she's not like me. It's not fair. She's only a year older than me but she's a head taller. She's only been doing this ladies' football lark a few weeks and yet she's already heaps better than me. I'd give anything to be in a proper team."

"Never mind, Squirt – sorry, *Jack*. There's more to life than boring old football, you know."

"Is there?" says Squirt, not sounding convinced.

"I have been through a profound psychic experience today, Jack."

"You what?"

"I have seen things no other living person has ever seen. I have stepped back in time."

"Your Tracy was right. You *are* having one of them funny turns."

"I am not! Oh it's no use, I'll never make you believe me. But you wait, I'll write it all down and then it'll be published as a book and it'll be a huge best seller and I'll get to go on *Wogan* and you'll sit at home watching me on the telly and you'll say, 'Gosh, I used to go round with Vicky Smith and I didn't appreciate her.' "

"I appreciate you like anything, you nutter. Why else would I be here? My sister won't be speaking to me now I've missed her big moment."

"I don't suppose my sister will be speaking to me either," I say uncomfortably. "Did she really play badly?"

"Lost all her concentration. Couldn't get it together at all. That Sue kept shouting at her."

"Oh dear." I'm not too keen to go back to the football match now. "Let's go for a stroll along the front, Sq – Jack."

It's still pretty misty so there aren't many people promenading about. It's all so different from the past.

"I'm so glad I'm in the present now," I mutter.

Squirt looks pleased, if a little puzzled. He tentatively takes my hand. We saunter along a little self-consciously.

"The coach doesn't leave till five. Would you like to go for a coffee or something?" He peers round and sees a big building with a dome. " 'The Fountains Ballroom, Bingo Hall and Cafeteria'," he reads. "It looks a bit old-fashioned but it'll do."

The Fountains looks as if it might have been impressive once upon a time. The fountains have fizzled out now. The white paint is peeling, there are several broken window panes, and the rubber plants in the dark foyer have lost all their bounce. There's music playing, a long-ago big band dance number that's still trying to limp along gamely.

"The cafeteria's through here," says Squirt. "Weird old dump, isn't it?"

"What's that music?"

"It's your actual ballroom dancing music. I expect they're having a tea dance for all the old grannies and grandads. Want to take a peek?"

Squirt is right. We open a door and peer at the big ballroom. It's still shabbily magnificent, with an enormous parquet floor in need of a polish and rickety gilt tables and chairs round the walls. There's even one of those revolving glass glitter balls set into the ceiling, making little stars of light in the dark room. They sparkle on the old age pensioners who are ducking and weaving to the old gramophone music, their backs straight, their arms up, their toes pointed.

Squirt chuckles appreciatively. I stare at the dancers, feeling touched. They might look funny but I don't really want to laugh at them. It's nice that they're hanging on to a bit of their past, coming to this shabby ballroom to foxtrot away from the future. In the dim light, speckled with stars, they don't even look that old.

I stare up at the glitter ball and watch the sparkles. Squirt is saying something but I don't want to listen in case he's taking the micky. He says it again and gives me a nudge.

"Hey! You gone off into a trance or something?" he complains. He knocks jokingly on my forehead. *"Is there anybody there?"*

The glitter ball sparkles and revolves, growing bigger and brighter. I'm whirling round with it, while the music gets fainter. I reach frantically for Squirt's hand to help me but he's no longer there. He's in the present – and I'm being whirled back to the past.

Seven

Rainbow lights dazzle my eyes. I blink but the lights are still there. I'm staring up at an ornate chandelier. I peer round desperately for Squirt but of course he's not here. This still seems to be the Fountains ballroom – there's the same high ceiling and domed windows – but we are in some sort of cubicle partitioned off by a large screen. My Victorian Mamma is sitting beside me, holding my hand, and there's a ghastly little man beaming at us behind a huge desk. He's one of those round smooth men who look as if they've been oiled in all their creases. He has a carefully combed little beard and a frilly shirt peeping out of his frock coat.

"Do you have any inkling why my daughter has suffered these alarming attacks, Dr Beamish?" Mamma asks anxiously.

"Calm yourself, Mrs Stathbridge. I know exactly what is the matter," says Dr Beamish, rubbing his oily pink paws.

I bet you don't, you horrid little man! How come I'm back in the past *again*? And why does it have to be right this minute? I don't like the look of Dr Beamish one little bit. I bet he's not a real doctor. I want to get out of here. I want to go home, a hundred years into the future!

"Young Miss Stathbridge is suffering from neurasthenia," Dr Beamish announces confidently, without giving me any examination at all.

"Oh dear," says Mamma. "Is it very serious, Dr Beamish?"

98

"Well, my dear Mrs Stathbridge, we must always take such complaints seriously. It can at times be positively dangerous in a young girl of delicate temperament. There have obviously been undue calls upon the little maiden's vitality and she is now in a state of severe sensitive exhaustion. However—" he adds, as Mamma gives a little moan, "you must not distress yourself, Mrs Stathbridge. Help is at hand. My new curative treatment has proved remarkably efficacious in similar circumstances. Of course, I recommend a very thorough and prolonged treatment as Miss Stathbridge's condition has become chronic."

"Whatever you say, Dr Beamish," says Mamma. "Although I do hope the treatment does not have to be *too* prolonged."

"Ah." Dr Beamish pauses delicately. "I wonder, Madam, if the fees are going to be a problem . . . ?"

"Oh, there is no problem at all where funds are concerned," says Mamma rather huffily, her cheeks going pink. "My husband owns a very large drapery establishment in one of the smartest suburbs of London. In fact he has even offered to send our daughter to the South of France if it would only cure her of these distressing attacks."

"Oh, no need to go abroad. In fact there are many invalids in Europe flocking to this very establishment. My reputation has gone far and wide, I do assure you."

"It is just that I will obviously have to remain with my daughter whilst she undergoes treatment and yet I cannot stay away from my husband and household for too long a period of time, as you will understand."

"Of course, Mrs Stathbridge. But there is no problem at all. After you have seen for yourself the ease and efficiency of the Hydropathic treatment and seen young Miss Stathbridge embarked upon a suitable course then you can establish her in one of the private suite of rooms attached to the Hydropath. They combine the luxury of a top hotel with the hygiene of the finest hospital, and should you care to make the additional provision I will be happy to provide a trained nurse to care for the young lady and a maidservant to perform all menial tasks. You need have no fears for your daughter. She will be as happy as a lark and soon regain her health. There! It's all settled."

"No!" I burst out. "Please, Mamma. I don't want to stay here. I don't want to have these treatments, whatever they are."

"But if Dr Beamish feels you would benefit, dear, then we must go along with his suggestions," says Mamma, holding my hand.

"But he'll suggest anything at all, just to get some money out of us," I hiss.

"Victoria!" says Mamma, obviously deeply shocked. "How can you say such a thing! Oh dear, whatever has got into you recently?"

"These mood changes are very common symptoms of a disturbed nervous system," says Dr Beamish. "Patients are often surly and hostile when they have formerly been of a markedly cheerful and polite disposition. Do not distress yourself, Mrs Stathbridge. I understand. I am a doctor. I deal with disordered nerves daily. Now, would you care to see the suite of rooms and reserve it for your daughter?"

"Mamma, please! Don't leave me here!"

"There is no need for us to take the rooms for the moment. I can stay in Fairhaven for a while yet and care for Victoria myself," says Mamma – and I give her a fervently grateful hug.

"As you wish," says Dr Beamish. He looks a little annoyed but he still oozes oily charm. "However, there is always a great demand for these rooms. There might not be a future opportunity . . . Still, I am sure you know best. Shall we begin the treatment then, Miss Stathbridge? If you would care to step this way?"

"Oh, not now!" I gasp.

"Don't be silly, Victoria. You must start the cure as soon as possible," says Mamma. "There's no need to be frightened, is there, Dr Beamish?"

"Of course not. I can assure you this is a perfectly natural treatment. You will feel no pain whatso- ever. Perhaps there will be just a little discomfort at first, before you get used to these methods – but generally our patients grow to love their treatments and greatly look forward to each ses- sion."

Oh help! It sounds like some kinky torture cham- ber. I cling to Mamma.

"You come with me, Mamma," I beg.

"Very well, my dear," says Mamma – but Dr Beamish intervenes.

"Oh, that will not be necessary, Mrs Stathbridge. Our treatments are conducted in absolute privacy in individual cubicles. There would not be room for anyone spectating."

"Indeed," says Mamma – and even she looks fussed now. "I am not sure . . . I do not care for the idea of my daughter being treated without a suitable chaperone."

"That's right, Mamma. Don't let him," I say frantically.

"I assure you, ladies, I do not conduct the treatments personally," says Dr Beamish. "One of my medically trained female attendants will perform the necessary highly specialized water treatments. I advise a brisk Friction treatment this morning, as this has proved remarkably efficacious for young ladies just blossoming into womanhood."

I shudder. Mamma surely can't believe a word this creep is saying. And yet she seems to be wavering.

"Mamma, please. You've got to stay with me!" I beg her. "I'm scared!" I edge closer to her and whisper in her ear. "I don't trust him. I'm terrified of what he's going to do to me. I'm sure he's just a dirty old man, even if he is a doctor."

Mamma looks alarmed.

"Don't be so silly, child. He looks an exceptionally clean man to me – and he's barely middle-aged," she whispers back to me.

Dr Beamish is flexing his fat pink fingers as if in anticipation.

"I don't mean he doesn't wash – I mean he'll try to touch me up," I hiss to Mamma. She gazes at me uncomprehendingly. "You know. He'll make a pass at me." Mamma still looks blank. Desperation makes me bold and I whisper a graphic description of my fears into her ear.

She gasps, chokes, turns practically purple.

I'm sure she'll whip me away to safety now. But she turns on me instead!

"Victoria! How could you ever come out with such disgusting degenerate sewer-talk!" Mamma hisses back at me. "Who on earth has been telling you such things?"

"Has the maiden purity been a little sullied?" Dr

Beamish enquires. "Do not fret, Mrs Stathbridge. My new curative water treatments restore health to the young mind as well as to the languid invalid body. Now, I will conduct Miss Stathbridge to the treatment rooms. I suggest you return for her at noon."

Mama straightens her hat, pulls on her gloves.

"Mamma, please!"

"Try to be a good sensible girl, Victoria. We must get you well as soon as possible," Mamma says. "I cannot believe you are actually my daughter sometimes when you behave in such a shameful fashion."

And with this she sweeps round the screen and out of sight. I stare after her bitterly. I don't know what to do now. If I shriek and scream then Dr Beamish might well tie me up and start his water tortures with increased relish. Maybe I can just make a bolt for it? But he's coming towards me, taking hold of my arm very firmly.

"This way, dear little Miss Stathbridge," he says.

I swallow hard. "Look. If there's any funny business at all, I'm warning you – I'll shout my head off."

"Please, Miss Stathbridge! I do assure you, I mean you no harm whatsoever. I am simply desirous of curing you by my wondrous natural water cure method. You are suspicious now because such methods are relatively new. I know that a hundred years from now such revolutionary treatments will be entirely taken for granted. There will be vast new Hydropaths in every town, nay, in every village. There will be vapour baths and sitz baths and sand baths and sun baths and the entire glorious variety of water baths and every man, woman – and even the

103

most nervous and delicate of maidens – will delight in abounding health and vitality. Medicine will be a thing of the past. Surgery will be unknown. There will be Hydropathic treatment universally and the name of Dr Beamish will be on everyone's lips."

"I know you're wrong," I say firmly, though I can hardly explain why I'm so definite. But I'm starting to waver a little myself. I can't stand him and I think his treatment sounds loopy, but maybe he isn't really a fumbly old creep as well. Maybe Victorian men do talk about maidens and blossoming bodies and all that junk just as a matter of course. Apart from the hand on my elbow he doesn't try to touch me or brush up close as he conducts me round the screen and across the long polished floor towards a semi-circle of chairs and several decorative potted palms. There are a cluster of patients in this waiting area. Many look alarmingly weak and frail, but they all straighten and smile as we approach.

"Good day, Dr Beamish!" they chorus.

He shows me to an empty chair and then wanders from patient to patient, giving them little words of encouragement. There's a poor thin girl sitting next to me, coughing almost continuously into her handkerchief. She seems frighteningly ill, though she does her best to smile at me in a welcoming manner.

"What's the matter with you?" I ask sympathetically.

"It's my lungs," she wheezes. "But I'm sure the water treatments are doing me some good. I have a chest pack put on me every morning, and then a sitz bath every afternoon. I think my breathing is definitely a little easier. Dr Beamish is doing all he can."

"Is he?" I say. "Wouldn't you be better going to a proper doctor, though?"

"I have consulted several doctors," she says. "They simply shake their heads and look grave. But Dr Beamish has given me new hope."

I look at her in anguish, wishing there was some way I could whizz her into the Twentieth century so she could get proper treatment in a modern hospital.

"Dr Beamish," I call desperately.

He comes to my side, after giving a reassuring smile and pat to the poor girl beside me.

"Yes, Miss Stathbridge. Are you seeing for yourself that some of my patients are actually grateful for the treatment I am offering them?" he says smugly.

"Dr Beamish, you want to be remembered in history, don't you? Well, I'll tell you how to do it. You've got to discover antibiotics."

"I beg your pardon, young lady?"

"Antibiotics. They're these chemical things you take and they stop infection. They could clear up this girl's illness, stop thousands and thousands of people dying."

"And where does one purchase these dubious cure-all chemicals? From Dr Quack's bargain stall in the market?" says Dr Beamish, and the patients waiting for his treatment smile obediently.

"Don't laugh at me. I *know* it's true. You can't buy them yet. You'll have to make them. I think you start off with penicillin. And I know where you can find that. In mould."

"In *mould?*"

"Yes, I know it sounds a bit crackpot, but it's honestly true. Get a very mouldy piece of bread or orange peel or something, you know what it goes like when it's mouldy, all blue and hairy—"

"And you're suggesting I should feed such fare to my patients?" says Dr Beamish. He looks round

105

at them, playing to his audience. "Would you find such morsels tempting, hmm?"

"You don't eat it just like that. You have to do all scientific things to it to turn it into pills. But it works wonders, truly."

"Oh it does, does it? And how do you know all these amazing scientific wonders, hmm? Do the leading medical men of the day consult you before starting their experiments?" he enquires sarcastically.

"They haven't started any experiments yet, that's the trouble. It'll be ages before they do. So you could get in first and make a real name for yourself and save countless people's lives, Dr Beamish."

"I see. You can look into the future and tell that this will happen?"

"Well. Yes," I say, reddening.

"Or perhaps you think you're *from* the future, charged with a knowledge that could cure the world's sick, is that it?" Dr Beamish goads.

"Yes, that's exactly it," I snap. "I know you're going to think I'm round the twist, but I *am* from the future and I'm right about antibiotics and I know one thing for certain sure, there aren't any Hydropaths in Fairhaven in my time. This building is a clapped-out ballroom filled with a lot of old dears hobbling through the Hokey-Cokey. The only place there's any water is the public toilets."

There's a little gasp from the assembled patients, but Dr Beamish remains jovial.

"Poor girl," he says, trying to touch my head. "Her condition is even worse than I feared. She is suffering from painful mental delusions. But never fear, Miss Stathbridge, we will effect a cure and restore you to your rightful maidenly demeanour."

106

A woman in a long white apron comes into the room.

"Ah, Miss Meadows. Ready for a new patient? I think Miss Stathbridge had better go first. She seems in dire need of treatment."

"No. Please. It's not my turn," I stammer, frightened again.

But Miss Meadows smiles at me reassuringly.

"Come along, dear. No need to feel nervous. It's all very beneficial," she says, and she takes me through a door and down a dark corridor.

"In here, if you please," she says, leading me into a little changing room, with one upright chair. There's a loose white gown hanging from a hook on the wall.

"Please remove your hat, pelisse, dress and boots. Loosen your stays, and put the modesty gown over your underclothing," she says. "Then step forward into the treatment room." She indicates another door at the other end of the changing room.

"No! I don't want to," I say, sounding as childish as little Peterkin – or Craig, my own little brother at home. I never thought I'd ever miss Craig, who is the least favourite of my brothers and sisters, but now I'd give anything to have one of our friendly romp-and-tickle sessions, with Craig laughing his little head off. I wonder if I'll ever get to hear his special spluttery chuckles ever again – and I start crying. I thought I'd got back to the present for good, but now I'm stuck here all over again.

"There now, Miss. Compose yourself. I promise you, the treatment doesn't hurt at all. Now, take your outdoor clothes off like I say. And the boots and your dress and your corsets. It would help if you could hurry up, because I've got to give a great many patients their treatments this morning, and some seem in a really sorry state."

"What if I still say no?" I say, sniffling.

"Then I shall have to fetch Dr Beamish," she says.

I gulp. "All right. I'll take my clothes off," I say, because the last thing I want is Dr Beamish's assistance.

She leaves me to struggle with my clothing. It takes ages because I'm still not used to all the fiddly little buttons and hooks. I get the corset things off but I don't know how I'm ever going to get back into them again. I put the white robe on and pull it tightly round me. It's warm enough in the changing room but I'm shivering. What are they going to do to me?

I move tentatively forward and push the other door a fraction. It swings open. Miss Meadows is waiting for me inside.

I look round the treatment room, and I'm in such a state that I give a hysterical snort of laughter. I'd been expecting some weird medieval torture chamber but it all looks so pathetic and amateurish and boring. There's another chair, a bucket, a lot of sheets and towels and a tiny flat bath no bigger than a washing-up bowl.

"How am I ever going to fit in that?" I say, giggling feebly.

"You step in and stand, Miss," says Miss Meadows stiffly, not appreciating my sudden hilarity. She takes one of the sheets and wraps it round me.

"Kindly remove your undergarments now," she says.

I do as I am told, while she holds the sheet up, averting her eyes. I have to shuffle sideways to place my camisole and petticoat and drawers and stockings on the chair, along with the white robe. Miss Meadows shuffles sideways too, holding the sheet aloft. It's as if we're doing the weirdest of dances. I have a mad desire to gallop round the room just to see if she'll follow.

"Now stand in the bath, if you please."

I look at the bath.

"But there's no water in it!" I say, stepping into it nevertheless.

"I appreciate that, Miss. The water is in the bucket," she says, and before I realize what she's doing she takes the bucket and sluices it all over me.

I give a loud shriek because it's icy cold.

"Stand still, please! And hold the ends of the sheet. I will now commence the rubbing treatment," she says, and she tightens the sheet all round me until I feel like an Egyptian mummy and then starts rubbing so vigorously she very nearly knocks me over.

It feels awful at first and I can still hardly catch my breath from the shock of the cold water, but after a minute or so I start to warm up.

"There! It's quite invigorating, isn't it?" she says, panting a little with the effort.

"I can think of ways I'd sooner be spending my time," I say.

"Do you feel a glowing in your inner organs?" she enquires. "The rapid friction will encourage your circulation, and when you have rich healthy blood pumping through your veins you will find your mind becomes pleasantly active and your mood amiable," she says.

"How long is it going to go on for?" I say, because the thought of being slapped about in a wet sheet the entire morning is not particularly jolly.

"I think five minutes would be ample for a first treatment," she says, rubbing away.

When she's finished she gives me a big rough towel to wrap round me. Rather to my irritation, I really do feel marvellous. Maybe I've misjudged old Dr Beamish after all. Even if his water treatment doesn't really cure it certainly makes you feel better.

"Is that it, then? Can I get dressed and go to wait for my mother?" I ask.

"I will go and consult with Dr Beamish," she says.

She returns in a minute or so, rolling up her sleeves.

"The doctor says you would benefit from a full water douche."

"What's that?" I say, starting to get nervous again.

"It is an application of water to the whole body."

"Cold water, I bet – and I've only just got warm again."

"Dr Beamish says that the double shock to your torpid constitution will be particularly beneficial."

"He would," I say. "Well, what happens? Do I stand in the bath and you tip the bucket over me again?"

"No, we move to the douching room," she says, indicating yet another door at the end of this treatment room.

The douching room is lined with tiles, although one or two have fallen off. There is a tap, a bucket, and a hose. It's like a home-made shower.

"If you would care to remove the towel I will commence the douche," she says. She produces a weird white mask which she puts over her eyes. "Be assured, I cannot see your person at all."

I drop the towel and try sticking my tongue out at her. She doesn't react.

"Are you ready, Miss? Stand in the centre spot, so that I know where to direct the pipe," she says.

I stand there like a lemon. She starts hosing me with water. It's cold and uncomfortable and she's doing it so slowly that we're going to be here till Christmas at this rate. I peer round the little douche room, wondering if I'll ever be able to get back to my own time and give an account of the mad medical practices of the late Victorian age. There's something gleaming in the wall. Something small and round, where one of the tiles has fallen off. I look closer. The gleam disappears for a split second and then returns. It's blinking! It's an eye, peering in at me. And I know whose eye it is too.

"Give me that," I say, and I grab the hosepipe from the masked Miss Meadows and play it full on the eye in the peephole. I hear a muffled shout. I grin.

"What are you doing, Miss?" says Miss Meadows, feeling in vain for the hosepipe.

"Just flushing away a minor irritation," I say. "Look, I've had enough of this. I'm going to dry myself and get dressed."

"But the douching isn't completed yet. Dr Beamish will be annoyed if you don't have the full treatment."

"I don't think he'll bother about it – not now," I say.

It takes me ages to get dry and properly dressed again. When I eventually emerge into the waiting room Dr Beamish is there, chatting to his poor patients. He looks a little under the weather himself now. His right eye looks very sore and inflamed.

"Did you enjoy your unusual supervision of my so-called treatment?" I say.

He flushes and looks away.

"I don't think you are really a suitable candidate for my water cures, Miss Stathbridge," he mumbles. "I will tell your Mamma that I regret that I cannot treat you further in this establishment."

"Yeah, and I'll tell my Mamma something too," I say threateningly.

But as I wait outside his crummy Hydropath I wonder if there really is any point telling tales to Mamma. She'll probably protest that I'm impure or immodest, as if *I've* done something wrong. And the other patients think Dr Beamish is wonderful. Maybe he spies on them, maybe he doesn't. But maybe it doesn't even matter if he makes some of them feel better. I think about that poor girl with her white drawn face and her terrible wheezing and I shiver.

"Victoria! Whatever are you doing here, my lamb?" Mamma bears down upon me, looking anxious. "How can Dr Beamish let you wait outside in this chill wind? You will catch your death of cold. What can he be thinking of?"

"He doesn't think I'll benefit from any more treatments, Mamma. And I don't want to go back there anyway. It's horrible. Some of the people are so ill. There was a girl not much older than me and she was coughing and wheezing and she was so thin that she really looked as if she were dying."

"Oh my goodness!" says Mamma, looking horrified. "And you were in close proximity to this poor girl?"

"Yes, we had a talk together and—"

"But this is unpardonable! You could have caught any disease. I had absolutely no idea Dr Beamish

112

would be treating consumptives. You must return to the lodgings and gargle with disinfectant solution. Oh child – to think that I insisted upon your treatment and wilfully abandoned you to a possible pit of infection! I shall never forgive myself. I have been worrying about it half the morning, walking backwards and forwards along the promenade, wondering how you were faring. My poor little pet."

Mamma presses me so hard against her that her corsets crackle. She bundles me back to Mrs Hubbard's and insists that I gargle so repeatedly that I breathe, smell and taste disinfectant for hours afterwards. I can't face Mrs Hubbard's cutlets and rice pudding. I lie down in my room and try to go to sleep. Nellie and the boys peep in at me, but I don't feel like talking.

I keep thinking of my own mum and dad and Tracy and Robert and Rachel and Craig. I think of my friends Jen and Karen and Alice. I think of Squirt. What's happening forward in the future? And how am I ever going to get there again?

"Victoria?" It's Mamma, rustling softly into my darkened room. "How are you, my dear?"

"I want to go home!" I say, and I burst into tears.

"My poor lambkin," says Mamma, gathering me into her arms. The smell of violets is somehow sweet and comforting now. "Well, so you shall, dear little one. I believe it was a mistake to come to Fairhaven. You are no better, George is missing his lessons, and little Peterkin is still coughing. We will all be better at home. We shall return tomorrow."

I slip down to the kitchen early next morning to see Mrs Hubbard. I cannot replace her crystal ball but I can help her foretell the future. I tell her I've had a curious detailed dream of what life will be like in a hundred years' time. I tell her about iceboxes in every home so that the milk doesn't go sour even in the hottest weather. I tell her about heat boxes that cook a meal from cold to piping hot in a minute. I tell her about machines that eat up all the dust and dirt with a greedy roar. I tell her about machines that wash all the clothes as white as white all by themselves. I tell her about machines that clean the dirty dishes at the press of a button.

She listens with her mouth open.

"But what would I do with myself if I had all these machines to do all the work?" she asks.

"Easy. There's another machine. The most magic of all. It sings to you and acts out stories and tells you jokes. It's like having your own non-stop music hall in your front parlour," I say.

"Oh my, Miss Victoria! What a vision of the future! If only it could ever come true," she says, sighing.

Eight

I'm at home. Only it isn't *my* home, even though this is 38 Westlake Road. This is a big three storey house, with a basement, and it's just like a museum crammed with exhibits. Lots of the ornaments are actually displayed in glass domes and cases. I think they all look hideous. I don't know which is worse:– the curly-headed little plaster tots with cutie-pie expressions, watched over by very pink plaster guardian angels with noses like Concord and wings to match, or the nauseating nature collage made out of hundreds of butterflies. No, maybe the worst of all the objects is the big glass case in the drawing room. It contains a large and slightly moth-eaten stuffed spaniel with its mouth clamped round a moulting game bird, its beady eyes popping. This is Rob Roy, ex-family pet, though he was a pampered city dog not up to molesting a budgerigar.

Rob Roy and his birdie friend give me the creeps so badly I can hardly bear to be in the same room, but little Peterkin positively adores him and begs to take him out of the glass case as a special treat. This is such a weird family that if anything untoward happened to little Peterkin they'd probably have him stuffed too and put on permanent display.

I can't *stand* little Peterkin – and George is almost as bad. I've got four more brothers too, all assembled here in the drawing room on our first evening back from the seaside. At first I get a bit confused and muddle them up.

"Why do you keep calling me Leo?" says Basil.

"And yet she called me Rupert just now," says Leo. "Is this one of your games, Victoria?"

"Victoria is still not herself, boys," says Mamma.

"You can say that again," I mutter.

I keep quiet until I've got each elder brother successfully sorted out. The eldest is Basil. He's about 18 or 19 and a right pain. Mamma tweaks his floppy silk tie and teasingly calls him a "masher". He's what I'd call a right poser. He keeps striking attitudes and peeking glances at himself in the looking glass. His trousers are embarrassingly tight. He'll do himself an injury if he isn't careful.

Basil works in the family shop with Papa. The next two brothers are usually away at some sort of boarding school but they've come home for half term.

"I'd have come home anyway. I've been jolly worried about you," says Leo.

I rather like Leo. He's 17 or so and he mightn't be as good-looking as Basil but he's very friendly and he makes quite a fuss of me.

"Young Ludovic's been worried about you too," says Leo, opening up a special suitcase.

At first I assume Ludovic's yet another brother but then I see Leo carefully lifting a ventriloquist's dummy with funny googly eyes out of the suitcase. Leo sits him on his knee.

"Yes, haven't we been worried about Victoria, Ludovic?" he says.

"I should say so, old man. Simply devastated to hear she's not been well," says Ludovic, his mouth opening and shutting. "How are you now, Victoria? You certainly look well, I must say. A very pretty girl, Leo, old man," and his glass eye winks saucily.

116

Leo's so clever that I almost believe Ludovic is real.

"You ought to go on the tele— I mean, the stage," I say, clapping.

"I'd love to do just that," says Leo. "But I'd need to work out a really original routine. There are so many ventriloquists in Music Hall. I'd love to think up a really *different* dummy."

"Easy peasy," I say. "How about a giant emu?"

"Goodness!" says Leo. "An *emu!* What an extraordinary idea, Victoria. Nobody else would think of that in a million years."

"Don't you be too sure," I say, grinning.

Rupert takes a turn working Ludovic, but he's nowhere near as clever as Leo. Rupert is very fat. When Blanche brings in a Victoria Jam Sandwich sponge, baked specially in honour of my homecoming, Rupert stuffs three big slices in a matter of seconds.

If Rupert is the fat brother then Frederick is the thin one. He's only about a year older than me and he doesn't go to boarding school because he's delicate. Mamma makes a great fuss of Frederick but Papa huffs and puffs and several times tells Frederick to pull his socks up and act plucky. Frederick doesn't really join in with the rest of the family. He sits on a footstool in a corner of the room and sketches us all.

"Really, Frederick, do you have to spend your time drawing like a girl?" Papa says irritably.

"Freddie's a girly-wirly," George sneers, and Peterkin joins in.

"Girly-wirly, Freddie-Weddie, girly-wirly, Freddie-Weddie," they tease and titter.

"Boys, boys!" says Mamma, clapping her hands.

"I shall ring for Nellie. George and Peterkin, it is time you were in bed."

While Nellie is dragging the two horrors out of the room I go over to Frederick.

"Can I have a look at what you've drawn?"

"If you like," he says shyly.

I flick through the pages of his sketch book.

"They're *ever* so good," I say, laughing.

Frederick's sketches are wonderfully surreal. He's drawn Basil with a peacock's head and a great tail bursting out of the back of his trousers. Leo has a jovial parrot's head while the dummy, Ludovic, has been given Leo's own features. Rupert has a big pink pig's head, of course – and George and Peterkin have ass's ears and are braying like donkeys.

"Oh gosh, what am I?" I say, giggling nervously as I turn the page.

I see a sketch of a demure Victorian miss with her own prim and pretty face – but her hands are little reptilian claws and there's a scaly tail peeping out of her petticoats.

"What am I? Some kind of lizard?"

"I've done you as a chameleon," says Frederick. "They're little lizards which can change colour. And I can't work out why, but you seem to keep changing just recently, Victoria."

"It's because Victoria's been ill, Frederick dear," says Mamma.

"No, it's not just that. It's something else," says Frederick. "It's almost as if she's changed inside."

"Well, that's only to be expected," says Mamma. "Victoria is growing up a little, becoming a young lady."

"She's still my little girl," says Papa. "And I've

missed you sorely, my dear. Come and sit on Papa's knee."

I approach him a little warily. I'm far too big to perch on anyone's knee, especially a strange Victorian gent with whiskers.

"Lord save us, she's acting shy of her own Papa!" he chuckles, and he pulls me onto his knee and joggles me up and down. I blush with embarrassment.

"There now, my pet. You've got the roses back in your cheeks at last. You're not going to have any more of these silly nervous fits, are you, my dear? I think you can go back to school tomorrow."

I nearly slide off his knee with shock.

"School?" I stammer. I can't go to a strict Victorian school where I won't know any of the lessons! "Oh Papa, do I have to?"

Papa fondles my foul ringlets.

"You've changed your tune somewhat, my sweeting," he says. "Not so very long ago I seem to remember the same little girl sitting on my knee and positively begging for the chance to go to this silly old seminary. You know I've never seen the need for girls to be educated. Oh yes, it's grand to have some ladylike accomplishments, but when it comes to all this scholarly nonsense I'm not sure I see the point of it. You'll just be screwing up your eyes over your schoolbooks and spoiling your looks.

"Yes, Papa," I say, nodding fervently, although his whole argument is incredible.

"What's the point of a little miss like you learning arithmetic, hmm? It's not as if you're going to be a banker," says papa, guffawing. "And studying this Shakespeare and all his plays, why, it's a waste of your time. You'd never want to see it at the theatre,

119

it'd be right above your head. No, a jolly Panto, that's the stuff for little girls."

My smile has become very set indeed. He really seems to believe all this crap. Still, I suppose it suits me to go along with it.

"So I don't really need to go to school, do I, Papa?"

"You can certainly give up this school nonsense next year, my darling. But your old Papa's paid a fortune for three further terms so we might as well get our money's worth. Stick it out another year, my dear."

"Papa, please. I'd really so much sooner stay at home."

His knee stills. The moustache twitches ominously.

"I am not accustomed to having my wishes opposed, Victoria. I allowed you to go to this school out of the kindness of my heart and I have paid a considerable sum to give you the dubious privilege of an education. Kindly show a little gratitude to your poor papa. Now, child, you will attend the seminary tomorrow morning. Do I make myself clear?"

"As crystal," I mutter, sliding from his knee.

"Now then! Do I detect a little sulkiness, Victoria?"

I struggle to keep my temper. I might have a right old go at my own dear old dad at home but I only dare go so far with this papa. I don't want to end up locked in my bedroom and fed on bread and milk, apparently the favourite household punishment for naughty children.

"I am just a little worried that I will have lost ground at school, Papa," I say, with all due reason. "I am not sure how I am ever going to catch up."

"You'll surprise yourself, my little girl," says Papa. "Don't look so worried. Your old papa doesn't much care how you do in all your book work, just so long as you write a nice clear hand and mind your manners. Remember the poem? 'Be good, sweet maid, and let who will be clever.'"

The Sweet Maid doesn't feel at all good next morning. She doesn't feel very clever either. She can't even manage to get into her school clothes properly. I thought my ordinary frocks were bad enough but this heavy navy serge school frock is perfectly foul and almost impossible to hook up. The bodice is like steel plating, there's a tight webbing waistband, and a stiff buckram collar throttling me round the neck. I can hardly move when I'm actually squeezed into this bizarre costume, especially as it's got a weird underskirt with a horsehair humpy thing at the front and a lot of little pennies sewn into the hem to weight it down. Perish the thought that anyone glimpses an inch of my black stockings!

I drag myself on to the landing in search of Nellie, who is wrestling with the boys.

"Do I look all right, Nellie?"

Nellie struggles to keep a straight face.

"Well, I've always thought those school dresses of yours a mite comical, Miss," she says. "But you've got your petticoats the wrong way round. The pad goes at the back."

"Oh yes, of course. I was wondering why I suddenly looked pregnant," I say, hitching violently at the humpy petticoat.

"*Miss!*" says Nellie, spluttering. "If your Ma hears you she'll wash out your mouth with carbolic soap."

Blanche serves me with a beautiful breakfast

121

of haddock and poached eggs and hot muffins, but I'm in such a state it tastes almost as foul as Nellie's soap. Mamma comments on my lack of appetite and I lay it on thick, saying truthfully enough that I feel dreadful – but Mamma is unrelenting.

"I daresay your spirits will revive once you are with all your special friends, my dear. Now come along. Fetch your bonnet and mantle. You don't want to be late your first morning back at Miss Gooding's."

I don't even know the way to this school. I'm not going to ask. Once I escape out the front door I've decided to slope off somewhere and play truant for the rest of the day. I'll have to find the Victorian equivalent of the Shopping Centre and hang out there. And I've snaffled several pennies from a china pig in my bedroom. It's no use looking for a can of coke and packet of crisps, but I think they sell lemonade and I can try one of those currant buns. It might even be fun to look around for a bit, see what the town used to be like. I'll keep clear of the market though, because that's where Papa has his famous shop.

But Mamma defeats my devious plans whilst I'm still hatching them.

"Victoria! Do stop daydreaming, child. Fetch your things. I shall accompany you to school. I wish to have a few words with Miss Gooding about your general health."

There's no way out of this. I trail along the road beside Mamma, my heart pounding hard against the iron cage of my corset. I can't even get interested in the changed vista of Westlake Road and its environs. I hunch my shoulders and stare at the pavement. I can't help looking up a little when we turn into Duke

Street because it's much busier and it still gives me a weird feeling seeing all these people wandering around in what looks like fancy dress. They all seem to walk surprisingly slowly – I suppose I've got used to seeing those speeded-up jerky old films of past times. The carriages and cabs and buses are so slow too – it must take ages to get anywhere. And it isn't half smelly! As we cross the road Mamma and I have to hitch up our skirts to stop them dragging in great steaming piles of manure. There's a little kid not much older than George sweeping it up. He's very thin and dirty and his clothes are ragged. I fumble for my piggy bank pennies and when Mamma isn't looking I press the pennies into his cold little hand.

We turn out of Duke Street and along Princes Avenue. It's all shops there now, but these seem to be private villas. There's a great big red building with a tower, a bit like a church, right at the end where the Regal Bingo Hall and Leisure Centre is now. As we approach I see a stream of navy serge flowing into the red brick entrance. This is obviously Miss Gooding's Select Seminary for Young Ladies.

"Oh look! It's Victoria!"

"Welcome back, old thing!"

"Oh jollification, jollification!"

There are three girls smiling at me and burbling the most amazing nonsense.

"Run and join Beatrice and Maud and Ethel," says Mamma, giving me a violet-scented kiss on the cheek. "Enjoy your day, my dear."

I am left with Beatrice and Maud and Ethel. I haven't a clue which is which. One is little and dumpy, one has very oddly prinked hair, and one is ultra giggly. They link arms with me and drag me into the red brick building, all chattering like mad. They sound so silly and affected and babyish at first. I long painfully for my own friends in the present, Jen and Karen and Alice. We go into a very formal classroom with several rows of rigidly arranged desks, and maps and religious pictures pinned on the walls. It looks very forbidding, but there's no teacher there yet and the girls carry on their casual nattering.

The dumpy one, who is Beatrice, boasts that she knows all the words of the latest hit song at the music hall and sings it for us. The prinked one, who is Maud, twiddles with her hair and asks if we like it behind her ears or with a few curls pulled forward. The giggly one, who is Ethel, tells us all about her cousin Ernest who actually squeezed her hand in a meaningful way last time they met!

"But you're very quiet, Victoria," says Beatrice. "Tell us all your news. Have you been very ill? My Mamma said you'd been to the seaside to take a water cure. Has it made you better?"

"That quack doctor couldn't cure a ham," I say. I think quickly. "Look. About my illness. I'm all right now, but it's affected the way I think a bit. I'll probably seem a bit different. And there's a lot of things I can't remember. So if I start making a right prat of myself doing something stupid give me a nudge, eh?"

They blink and look bewildered, but nod readily enough.

I need so many nudges through morning school that I expect my sides are black and blue. We have Prayers first, and they seem to go on for ever. But when we begin the first lesson, arithmetic, I start saying further silent prayers because I'm going to need the help of the Almighty to cope. I thought our maths at my school was hard enough but this stuff is even worse. Solid geometry and analytical and geometrical conics! You what?

I sit in a stupor while this fierce lady teacher in black chalks madly on the blackboard. Then she hands round some very pretty red marbled notebooks and quill pens and sets us all five problems on the board. It takes me all the lesson to copy out the sums with this scratchy pen and horrible blobby brown ink – let alone come up with anything like any answers.

"Victoria!" the teacher exclaims, peering at my work. "Whatever is amiss? You are usually my star pupil. I know you have been unwell – but I was not aware that you had suffered from Brain Fever! This is disgraceful. You have not attempted a single answer. Well, my girl, you will take this book home and work on the answers there. Report back to me first thing tomorrow morning, do you understand?"

I understand only too well. Whichever life I'm leading I seem to be in difficulties over arithmetic.

History is slightly less humiliating because we don't have to write anything down, we just have to sit and listen. I am prodded in the back with a ruler because I am slouching instead of sitting up straight and I am tutted severely when I try a tentative whisper to Beatrice. The history teacher is old and boring, very much like Old Maxy, my history master. She's even got his moustache. But the history she teaches makes me squirm. It's all about our glorious British Empire and how we have conquered the entire world and isn't it all jolly and splendid. She keeps pointing at all the pink on the map of the world which denotes our great dominion.

It's a relief when we have a break. We all

drink big beakers of milk and eat squashed fly biscuits.

To my great surprise the next lesson is Wood-carving. It's taught by this pretty young woman with a tortoiseshell clasp in her hair and a long flowing purple gown.

"Isn't she wonderful? I've got such a pash on her," Beatrice breathes fervently.

"She's all right, but I much prefer Susannah," says Maud.

"Oh yes, we've got Susannah next, for calisthenics. Oh jollification, jollification," Ethel enthuses.

Calisthenics turns out to be rather dopey arm-swinging, marching exercises organized by the Vice Captain of the school, Susannah. Beatrice and Maud and Ethel and the other girls in my class seem to think Susannah the supreme star of the school. *I* think she's a scream, a strapping girl with a swaggering stride. She demonstrates the exercises with panting enthusiasm, her long blonde pigtail thumping her back. Her face turns very pink above her tight white collar and the seams of her serge frock strain to contain her. It's so daft doing exercises in these clothes. I try to picture Susannah in sensible shorts with her hair shorn and realize she'd be the spitting image of Sue, the captain of Tracy's football team.

Beatrice and Maud and Ethel still sing Susannah's praises as we walk across the school yard afterwards, albeit breathlessly.

"She's so athletic," says Maud. "She plays hockey and lacrosse."

"And did you know, her papa is going to buy her a bicycle!"

"Oh fancy! I do hope we see her ride it."

126

"Oh jollification, jollification! Susannah on a bicycle!"

"What's so special about a bicycle?" I say, starting to get irritated.

"Why, Victoria! I think it's splendidly plucky of Susannah. I know men can ride bikes – my cousin Ernest is a member of a cycling club as a matter of fact – but it's highly dangerous for girls."

"Rubbish," I say. "I can ride a bicycle."

They stare at me.

"You might have been ill, Victoria, but that's still no reason to tell silly untruths," says Maud.

"I *can*. Where's someone's bike? I'll show you."

"Monsieur Bertillon rides his bicycle to school. It's in the shed. Oh jollification, jollification, are you really going to ride it?"

"Don't, Victoria. You know you'll only fall off and hurt yourself dreadfully," Beatrice hisses.

I take no notice. I go to the shed and open the door. I see the bicycle. Oh no! It's a Penny Farthing, one of those weird old bikes with a huge front wheel. But I can't back out now. I'll show them.

I wheel the Penny Farthing out of the shed with great difficulty, because it's so heavy and unwieldy. It takes me several goes to get on the thing, and once I do I fall off. But I don't give up. I hitch my skirts round my thighs and cling to the handlebars and set off. I veer wildly to the right, I wobble frantically, I do a zig-zag, I go over a stone and almost go flying, but I stay on it somehow. I ride that Penny Farthing all the way round the school yard – and Beatrice and Maud and Ethel cheer!

Nine

Mamma is waiting as I come out of the school gates at half past three. She doesn't look particularly pleased.

"Come along, child! I'm afraid there's no time for you to dawdle with your friends. We must go to the shop immediately."

"The shop? Which shop?" I ask, waving goodbye to Beatrice and Ethel and Maud.

"Papa's shop!" says Mamma, sighing at my stupidity. "We have to pick out two lengths of material, plus trimmings, buttons, tapes and any ornaments – and at five o'clock I have arranged for Miss Marshall to give you a proper fitting at home for *two new frocks*." Mamma hisses the last three words and glares at me.

I blink back at her, not twigging what she's on about.

"Don't try to look so innocent, Victoria! Blanche and I unpacked the last of the trunks this morning and I discovered your rose silk and your lilac muslin crushed at the bottom in an appalling state. Dirtied, torn, totally unwearable! Whatever have you been doing, child?"

"I haven't been doing anything, Mamma," I say with truthful indignation.

"But you look as if you have some idea how your two best dresses have been ruined," says Mamma.

I hesitate – but much as I can't stand George and Peterkin I'm not a sneak. I shake my head – and so

128

Mamma gives me a long lecture on carelessness. It's so boring that I can't stifle a yawn.

"Are you very weary, child?" Mamma says, her tone softening. "Did you find your day at school very tiring? Perhaps I should not have dragged you straight off to the shop. Yet you must be supplied with new dresses as soon as possible, especially with the party season nearly on us. Here child, take my arm."

I hook into Mamma and she hurries us along. It's getting dark already and there's a nasty damp grey mist. Mamma stops to button my mantle right up under my chin.

"There! That should keep you cosy. We must hurry, dear. I am afraid there is going to be a fog."

All the market stalls are eerily lit by naphtha flares. The stallholders shout out cheerily in the damp air. One of them calls me Curlylocks and I smile and give him a wave. Mamma gives me a little shake, appalled, and rushes me towards the genteel sanctuary of Messrs A C Stathbridge and Co., Ladies' Hatters, Milliners, and Fancy Drapers.

It's an amazing place, the window positively crammed with thousands of items, all neatly labelled and priced in an exquisite copperplate hand. It's like one of those puzzle picture books where you have to count all the objects. The shop is blazing with light from four huge gas lamps outside and special fancy gaseliers inserted into the ceiling at frequent intervals. A very servile man in a frock coat leaps to attention when he sees us and ushers us to Papa's special chamber. As we open the door Papa seems to be dozing gently in his chair, a newspaper in his lap – but by the time we are in his little office he has jerked into action and is apparently poring over the account books.

Mamma explains the reason for our unexpected visit and Papa nods at her and tuts at me and rubs his hands briskly together.

"Right, my dears. Come with me," he says, opening his door and striding forth.

As he struts through each department the assistants bob into action, giving him nervous nods of the head. The material department is at the side of the shop. There are great bolts of material stacked right up to the ceiling and a large polished counter. There are two young boy assistants at either end of the counter. Before he senses our approach the smallest boy rolls a marble at top speed down the polished counter and into a glass jar turned on its side. It gives a satisfying rattle as the "goal" is scored. The boy gives a yelp of triumph – and then a yell of anguish as Papa reaches out and gives him a furious smack about the head.

"How dare you play games when you should be attending to your duties!" Papa bellows.

"I'm sorry, sir. It won't happen again, sir," the small boy gabbles, but the moment Papa turns back to Mamma the boy pulls a comical face, crossing his eyes and waggling his tongue. When his eyes straighten he sees I've been watching. He looks scared. I quickly pull a face back, one of my particular specialities, eyes dragged down and nose turned up into a snout. The boy splutters helplessly. There's something so *familiar* about him.

"Victoria? Whatever are you doing to your eyes?" says Mamma, turning to me.

"Oh, I think I have a slight speck in them, Mamma," I say demurely.

"Well, rectify matters immediately, child. I need your full attention. We have to choose this material."

Papa directs both boys to pull down bolt after bolt of cloth. They clamber up and down the stepladder like a pair of monkeys. Papa barks confusing orders: "Not the chintz, you foolish boy! The muslin, the muslin. Not *that* muslin, as if young Miss Stathbridge would ever wear such a colour! The primrose, if you please." The boys scramble about, bumping into each other.

"Out the way, Tich," says the bigger one.

"My name's *not* Tich," the little one says indignantly.

I lean on the counter, staring at him.

"What *is* your name?" I whisper.

He looks surprised but he draws himself up to his full height and squares his puny shoulders.

"My name's Jack Philip Andrew Norris, Miss," he says.

"Tich," jeers the other boy.

"You call me Tich and I'll punch your face," Jack Philip Andrew threatens under his breath.

"Squirt!" I say delightedly.

"Beg pardon, Miss?"

"I – I've just realized. I think I know a – a relation of yours."

"I don't think so, Miss," he says doubtfully. "My family live the other side of London. I'm just apprenticed here to your Pa."

"Well, I have a feeling you might settle in this area. And get married and have children. And they'll have children. And *they'll* have children. And one of the boys might even be named after you," I say.

"Victoria? Whatever are you saying to one of

Papa's boys?" says Mamma, distracted from examining a bolt of material with Papa.

"We were just having a little conversation, Mamma," I say hurriedly.

"You were talking to Miss Stathbridge, lad?" Papa says, frowning. "Impertinence!"

"Oh no, Papa. It was my fault entirely," I say. "Jack – er, Mr Norris here, was being particularly helpful."

"That I very much doubt," says Papa. "Bring down the Chinese silk, young Norris, and look lively about it."

Poor Jack looks lively. We don't get a chance of further conversation. Mamma keeps holding swathes of cloth under my chin to see if they enhance my colouring and drape in a satisfactory manner. She asks me which I prefer but as I think they're all pretty hideous I just shrug silently. I'm going to look ridiculous whatever we choose, like a bridesmaid who's lost the wedding. Mamma eventually plumps for an apple green watered silk and a white organdie. Papa himself wields the scissors, cutting the material with one small expert snip and then tearing it across with a wonderful blaring rip.

"Parcel it up neatly in brown paper, boy," he orders Jack.

We cross to another counter and Mamma selects pink silk ribbon to trim the green and a sky blue sash to wear with the white organdie. We choose tiny grass green buttons and little seed pearl buttons and several cards of hooks and eyes and some vicious looking stiffeners and armpit shields and goodness knows what. I had no idea that all these bits and pieces went into the making of two dresses. Jack is kept busy parcelling these all up too.

"We must take the materials with us," says Mamma. "I want Miss Marshall to get started on Victoria's dresses as soon as possible."

"I'll send the boy along with you," says Papa. He peers worriedly out of the window. "It's getting very foggy. Better make haste and take the bus."

I'm pleased that Jack is coming with us, though he has to stagger several respectful paces behind us, his arms weighed down with paper parcels.

"Shall I carry one for you?" I offer.

"Victoria!" Mamma hisses, scandalized.

I raise my eyebrows apologetically at Jack – and he grins back. We pick up the bus at the opposite end of the market. Only of course it's not my idea of a bus with a proper engine. This bus is pulled by a horse. The driver sits up at the top, with several seats beside him.

"Oh, can we sit up at the top, Mamma?" I ask.

"Don't be ridiculous, child," says Mamma.

We have to sit inside the bus, crammed on to the grubby blue velvet seats with a lot of other passengers. Lucky Jack gets to balance up on top. It's horribly airless inside the bus, and there's nasty wet straw on the floor that tickles my ankles. We keep stopping to disgorge passengers and pick up more, and as the fog thickens and it gets properly dark, our pace gets slower and slower. Mamma keeps trying to peer out of the tiny windows to see where we are.

"I hope Nellie didn't take the boys for too long a walk," she says anxiously. "I don't like to think of my little Peterkin with his delicate chest out in a nasty peasoup fog."

"Mamma, now that I'm going to have these two new dresses, the green one and the white one, I won't still be wearing the pink and the lilac, will I?"

"Well, they might just wash up, but they'll never be the same again. I daresay you might wear the lilac as a third best, but the pink is only fit for the scrap basket."

"Could I give the frock to someone instead of scrapping it, Mamma?"

"But whoever would want a discarded torn frock, Victoria?"

I take a deep breath. "Nellie."

"Nellie!"

"Please, Mamma. She'd like it so much, I know she would."

"But she could never wear such a dress. It's silk! Nellie is a common servant girl. She's never worn silk in her life."

"I know. That's why I'd so like to give it to her."

"When would she ever find a use for it? She can hardly wear torn pink finery when she's scrubbing the nursery floors or bathing little Peterkin."

"She could wear it in her free time – what little she gets," I say. "Oh *please*, Mamma."

"Really child. There's no need to get so passionate about it. I'm sure Nellie would make far better use of one of your school serges that is now too small for you."

"I want to give her the pink silk. *Please.*"

"Oh how you plague me, child," says Mamma. "Very well. You may give Nellie the pink silk if you really must."

"Oh *thank* you, Mamma," I say, giving her arm a squeeze.

"What an odd little creature you are, Victoria," says Mamma. "You get such strange fancies nowadays. Sometimes I feel you're a total stranger."

"That's the way I feel too, Mamma," I say.

"I believe we're getting near Westlake Road now," says Mamma. "Come child, we must alight. Alert the conductor."

We stumble out of the bus into the fog, which seems far thicker here. Jack scrambles down from the top of the bus, winding his scarf round his face.

"You need to protect yourself from the fog, Miss Victoria. And you too, Ma'am," he says cheerily.

"Quite right, young Norris. Put your handkerchief over your mouth, Victoria," Mamma commands. "Now, we must step lively. This way. No, wait a minute. Is it this way or that way? Where are we? I cannot even work out which side of the road we are on."

"Allow me, Ma'am," says Jack. "This way. You follow close behind. We've just turned the corner, see. Your house is up here, on the right."

He leads us along confidently. We see a flare bobbing up ahead, and when we get close we can see it's another boy leading an anxious-looking old lady.

"You need a torch, mate," he says to Jack. "Then you can charge a shilling to get them home – more if it's a long journey and they're proper toffs."

Jack laughs. Mamma sucks in her breath crossly – but when we reach the front door of number 38 she turns to Jack, fumbling in her reticule, the dinky little purse she carries about with her.

"Here, boy." She hesitates. "Here's . . . a sixpence for your trouble. And a penny for the bus fare back."

"Thank you, Ma'am. Will I carry the parcels round to the back for you?"

"If you please, boy. Thank you for your trouble. Now, come along, Victoria."

I hang back. "Thank you very much for dragging all this way with us, Jack," I say, and I do my best to shake his hand, although he still has to clutch tight at the parcels.

"My pleasure, Miss Victoria."

"That sounds so stupid. Why don't you call me Vicky?"

"Right, Miss . . . Vicky."

"I'll try and come in the shop again soon."

"Yes, you do that. I'll look out for you."

"I wish I could have a game of marbles with you."

"Here." He reaches in his pocket and then presses something into my hand. "It's my lucky King marble. Maybe it'll bring you luck too."

"Whatever are you doing, Victoria?" Mamma calls from the top of the steps. "Come along at once, child!"

"Bye, Jack! Thanks ever so much," I whisper and then rush up the steps, the marble clenched tightly in my hand.

"Straight upstairs, Victoria," says Mamma, as Blanche opens the door to us. "I want you to take off that damp school dress and wrap yourself in flannel. You can have tea in your dressing gown. I'll have it sent up to you. And then Miss Marshall should be here for the dress fitting."

"But she surely won't come out on a foggy night like this, Mamma?"

"Of course she will! We require those dresses urgently. I want her to start stitching this evening."

"Won't she mind working those sort of hours?"

"Miss Marshall is a sensible businesswoman. Therefore she has to do business – otherwise she may very well end up in the workhouse."

136

"But it's all so unfair! What work am *I* going to do?"

"Work? Don't be ridiculous, Victoria. You are a young lady. Your papa owns a very profitable and respectable drapery establishment. There is no need for you to work for your living."

"So there's always one rule for the rich and one rule for the poor."

"Well, of course there is," says Mamma. "We must all know our places and keep to our stations. Now do run along and take off those damp things, child, and stop this silly arguing."

I give up and do as I am told. I put my head round the nursery door when I get upstairs. Nellie is crawling about on the rug with George and Peterkin, playing a game of battles with the lead soldiers.

"You're back at last, Miss," says Nellie. "How did your day at school go? All right, was it?"

"Well. Not really. But never mind that now. Mamma took me to buy some dress material because she got in a right old state about my pink and lilac frocks. You know."

"Did you tell on us?" asks George, looking worried.

"Mamma will be cross," says Peterkin, and he sucks a toy soldier anxiously.

"Don't suck that! It's lead. You mustn't ever," I say, snatching it away. "Of course I didn't tell. Who do you think I am?"

"You're our sister and you usually tell tales on us," says George.

"Well, I didn't this time, so ha ha," I say. "Anyway, Nellie, I asked Mamma if you could have one of the dresses. She says you can have the pink one. I know it sounds awful, palming off my old things on

137

to you, and maybe you won't want it anyway as it's a bit torn, but I thought I'd offer it anyway. Would you like it?"

"Oh Miss!" says Nellie, her eyes huge. "Oh Miss, you don't mean it, do you?"

"Of course. Come and get it."

I take her into my bedroom and give her the crumpled pink silk frock. She holds it very carefully in her hands, and then stoops and rubs her cheek against the soft silk.

"Oh Miss," she says again, and then she hurries out of the room, giving a little whoop of joy.

I go to the window to draw my curtains. I stare out into the swirling grey fog and shiver. I hate fog. I remember searching for Madame Rosalie in the Fairhaven fog. Oh, how I wish I hadn't found her now!

I lean my head against the windowpane and squeeze my eyes tightly shut as I think about home and my family and friends. I got back once – I've simply got to do it again. If only I had some idea how to work the magic mechanism of these time switches.

I start crying like a baby. Then when I go to rub my eyes I find I'm still clutching Jack's marble. It's a beautiful big crystal marble. I hold it towards the gas light up above and see a strange rainbow dazzle. I twist the marble in my fingers and the rainbow spins. I stand and stare, totally absorbed. I whirl round in my wet skirts, so that I'm spinning too.

Wait a minute. Was that a timid knock at my door?

"Is there anybody there?" I call.

"It's only me, Miss," says Nellie, opening the door and showing me how lovely she looks in the pink silk dress. She twirls round – but I am still

138

twirling too. I can't seem to stop. The rainbow still swirls. I can hardly see Nellie now. There's a roaring in my ears. The floor is tilting sideways. I am tilting too, tumbling over and over. I stare into the crystal marble and just for an instant a face stares back at me – my face. And then the rainbow flashes brighter and brighter, the colours whirl, soon they're just a white shimmer, a great bright white splendour and I flounder forwards, faster and faster, and then suddenly I bang my head and the white goes black.

"Mind her head! Lay her down *gently*. She's in a bad enough state as it is. Out cold! I don't know what you've been giving her to drink, young Jack, but I think it's absolutely disgraceful!"

"I swear I didn't give her anything to drink, Mrs Smith. We never even had that cup of coffee. Vicky just came over queer all of a sudden. She stared up at this light and then her eyes went funny and she collapsed. I couldn't get through to her at all. It was as if she was in a trance. I managed to walk her back to the football pitch but it was as if she was sleepwalking all the way – and then she slept all the journey home on the coach. I don't know what's the matter with her. Maybe we ought to call a doctor."

"She's going to *need* a doctor by the time I've finished with her! Oh Mum, it's so unfair. I was so worried about her that I played like a pudding and now if I don't watch out Squirt's sister will be in the team and not me. She scored two goals! And it's all Vicky's fault."

"Stop going on about your silly football, Tracy. I think Jack's right. Ring for the doctor."

"Don't let him hose his water at me!" I say in a panic – and I open my eyes. I blink. I stare. There's

139

Squirt sitting beside me on my bed. There's Mum, Dad, Tracy, Robert, Rachel and Craig, all looking down at me worriedly. I'm back! Back in my own bedroom in the present!

"Oh, how wonderful!" I gasp.

"You think it's wonderful that I'm probably going to be dumped from the team?" says Tracy furiously. "I'd sink back into unconsciousness if I were you!"

"No fear! Hang on to me, all of you! Don't let me get sucked back."

"I'll hold you, Vicky. There now. I've been looking after you all afternoon."

"Dear old Tich."

"You what? Here, Squirt's bad enough, but Tich is worse."

"Sorry! It's just – did you ever have a great-grandad who worked in a draper's shop? He gave me his special marble."

"She's raving! Call that doctor right away," says Dad.

"I think she's just playing one of her games again," says Robert.

"She's a bad girl, isn't she?" says Craig.

"I think she's good and I love it when she plays Victorian games with me," says Rachel.

"I hope I never play those games again, Rachel!"

"Are you really all right now, Vicky?" says Mum.

"Yes, I'm fine. It's just I had this weird psychic experience." I see their expressions. "Okay, call it a dream if you like. It doesn't matter. The only thing that matters is that I'm back and it's all over and it's so great to see you all again!"

I sit up properly and give them all a big hug. Tracy hisses at me and Squirt kisses me and the others simply sigh and shake their heads.

140

"I don't know what I'm going to do with you, our Vicky," says Mum. "I don't know what you're going to get up to next."

"Neither do I," I say. "That's the trouble!"

Stevie Day
Series

JACQUELINE WILSON

Supersleuth	£2.25	☐
Lonely Hearts	£2.25	☐
Rat Race	£2.25	☐
Vampire	£2.25	☐

An original new series featuring an unlikely but irresistible heroine – fourteen-year-old Stevie Day, a small skinny feminist who has a good eye for detail which, combined with a wild imagination, helps her solve mysteries.

"Jacqueline Wilson is a skilful writer, readers of ten and over will find the (Stevie Day) books good, light-hearted entertainment."

Children's Books December 1987

"Sparky Stevie"   *T.E.S. January 1988*

ARMADA

SCRAMBLED
L·E·G·S

JAHNNA N. MALCOLM

Rocky: hot tempered
Mary Bubnik: worst dancer ever
Gwen: shortsighted and sharp-tongued
McGee: ice-hockey fanatic
Zan: head permanently in the clouds

Five friends at Deerfield's Academy of Dancing. What do they have in common?
THEY ALL HATE BALLET.

Follow the hilarious exploits of the gang, and their continual battle against the Bunheads, in this exciting series of 6 books:

ARMADA

All these books are available at your local bookshop or newsagent, or can be ordered from the publisher. To order direct from the publishers just tick the title you want and fill in the form below:

Name _____

Address _____

_____

Send to: Collins Childrens Cash Sales
          PO Box 11
          Falmouth
          Cornwall
          TR10 9EN

Please enclose a cheque or postal order or debit my Visa/ Access –

   Credit card no:

   Expiry date:

   Signature:

– to the value of the cover price plus:

UK: 60p for the first book, 25p for the second book, plus 15p per copy for each additional book ordered to a maximum charge of £1.90.

BFPO: 60p for the first book, 25p for the second book plus 15p per copy for the next 7 books, thereafter 9p per book.

Overseas and Eire: £1.25 for the first book, 75p for the second book. Thereafter 28p per book.

ARMADA